IN THE NAME OF THE FATHER

ADAM CROFT

GET MORE OF MY BOOKS FREE!

To say thank you for buying this book, I'd like to invite you to my exclusive *VIP Club*, and give you some of my books and short stories for FREE.

To join the club, head to adamcroft.net/vip-club and two free books will be sent to you straight away! And the best thing is it won't cost you a penny — ever.

Adam Croft

For more information, visit my website: adamcroft.net

BOOKS IN THIS SERIES

Books in the Knight and Culverhouse series so far:

To find out more about this series and others, please head to adamcroft.net/list.

1

Isabella Martin stood rooted to the spot as Father Joseph Kümmel's eyes bore into hers. For a while, he said no words. He didn't need to.

She'd been considering her escape from Hilltop Farm for some time. Recently she'd made the grave mistake of voicing her doubts to another member of the community. She'd thought she could trust her, considered her a friend. But now she was standing in front of the man who'd started this, who'd brought them all here, and expected her to repent for her sins.

'Isabella, do you ever plan your own death?' the man said, his deep Germanic tones rumbling as he spoke.

The farmhouse smelt damp and musty, as it always did at this time of year. The room felt oppressive, little light sneaking in through the small, high windows. Although she stood alone, facing the seated Father Joseph across his desk, she felt a thousand eyes upon her. The building was known as the chapel, although Isabella had long since rejected it as such in her mind. To her, it was now just another farmhouse. In any case, it felt more like a crypt than a chapel.

She swallowed, her mouth dry, struggling for something to say.

'No... No, I don't.'

Father Joseph smiled. It wasn't a happy smile, but the knowing twinkle of a parent whose child has just told them they're going to be an astronaut when they grow up.

'Do you not find that odd? After all, let's face it: you're going to die. We all are. Do you not think it important to plan ahead and take control over that event?'

Isabella clenched her teeth. Control was something she'd lacked for a long time, something she'd gradually come to realise she was missing. And here was the man she held responsible, urging her to take control, telling her it was within her power. Had she been wrong all along? Had Father Joseph been guiding her nobly, the only resistance coming from within herself?

'It... It's not something I've ever thought about,' she said, desperate to gauge Father Joseph's mood and thoughts from the look in his eyes.

'Do you not think it is time to think about it?' he said, cocking his head slightly to one side. He stayed silent, looking at her. Isabella could tell he was going to say no more and felt compelled to speak next.

'I'm not sure what you mean.'

Father Joseph smiled again.

'Child, you have a strong character. A strength of will. It is that strength of will that compelled you to express your doubts, to consider leaving the community. Do you see now that you were misguided in that sentiment?'

Isabella nodded, unable to express any words. She tried to work out whether he was angry or empathetic, but couldn't.

'You are not to blame, Isabella,' he said, as if reading her mind and wanting to answer her question. 'It is perfectly natural for someone as strong willed as you to doubt. But you are also well aware of what dark forces have planted that doubt, are you not?'

She nodded again. The word wasn't one that was ever spoken within the community. No matter how removed Isabella had felt from this place recently, she still felt a cold shiver down her spine whenever she even considered it.

'Which is why it is time for you to take control, Isabella. You are in charge of your own destiny. You make every decision in your life through free will. It is your free will that brought you here, that put you under the wing of God's love. You are a person in control. Do you want those dark forces to consume you from within, to take that control away from you?'

Isabella shook her head, slowly at first.

'No... No.'

'Then you must take the ultimate control,' he said, sliding a coffee mug across the desk towards her with the tips of his fingers. 'You must make the decision. Take the step that most people will never have the strength of character to take.'

Isabella looked down at the coffee mug. It looked like any cup of coffee, except there was no steam. She looked back up at Father Joseph, seeing that his eyes had never left hers.

'I... I can't,' she said. 'I don't want to.'

'It is not you speaking, Isabella. You want to take control. You want to make this choice.'

'No... No. I don't. I can't,' she said, her voice faltering.

Father Joseph clenched his jaw. Isabella heard two footsteps to her side. She turned her head and saw the faint but familiar frame of Nelson, one of Father Joseph's closest confidants. His eyes were milky and tense, his black skin still disguised in the shadows. She caught a glint of light that flashed below and just to the left of Nelson. It was only for a moment, but enough to make her realise that he was holding a gun in his right hand.

Isabella looked back at the coffee mug.

She recalled the stories one of the other members of the community had told her. Legend was that those who transgress are sometimes made to prove their devotion to the community and to Father Joseph. Long before Isabella had come to the farm, a male member of the community was apparently handed a gun by Father Joseph and told to kill one of the two of them. The man had lifted the gun to his own temple and pulled the trigger, only to find the gun hadn't been loaded. From that point on, having proven his devotion, the man had lived the life of a king. Isabella didn't know his name, or what had ultimately happened to him, nor did she know anyone who'd ever met him. But the story remained powerful, indelible on her consciousness.

Was this what was happening here? Was this simply a harmless mug of cold coffee, intended to be a make-or-break moment for her? Either way, she now knew what the alternative was. She glanced back at Nelson, herself almost able to feel the cold steel of the gun.

She extended her arm, her elbow popping as she did so, and took hold of the coffee cup. Slowly, she lifted it to her lips and drank.

It was definitely coffee, she knew that much. Cold coffee. Knowing the taste would be unpleasant, and only wanting to experience it once, she slugged back the mug's contents in one.

Within seconds of putting the mug down, she could feel the butterflies in her chest and throat. Her neck tightened as she began to gasp for breath. Time seemed to slow, her legs buckling from under her as her stomach began to heave, her body shivering as it began to convulse. Without warning, she vomited, the stream of liquid splattering across the concrete floor of the farmhouse, masking the sound of her losing control of her bowel and bladder.

Gradually, everything faded, became black.

2

Jack Culverhouse sat in the armchair in his living room, as he had all night, looking at the clock. It was almost nine-thirty in the morning and he ought to be at work, but work could wait.

He'd just handed a big case over to the Crown Prosecution Service. It was the attempted murder of an investigative journalist who'd been about to expose a local political scandal and cover-up. He figured he was due a break. Besides which, he'd just seen his thirteen-year-old daughter for the first time in almost nine years, having tried to track her down all over the world before finding out she'd been living in the same county the whole time.

His wife, Helen, had disappeared with Emily in the dead of night all those years ago and had only recently come back on the scene. He had no idea why — she'd become a completely different person and now seemed hell bent on causing arguments and frustration. She'd led him a merry dance, right across Europe, trying to track her down and see his daughter again. But, through it all, Emily had been living with Helen's parents barely a few miles up the road. Helen'd had almost as little contact with her as Jack had.

When Emily had got in touch with him yesterday evening, it had been the last thing he'd expected. He'd been to see her that week at the skatepark near where she'd been living, hoping to catch a glimpse of her but not intending on speaking to her. That had all changed as soon as he saw her.

The welcome he got had been less than enthusiastic. Although Emily had recognised him immediately, she'd made it crystal clear that she had no desire to see him or spend any time with him.

But that seemed to have been a momentary flash in the pan.

He'd called her back as soon as he received her text just before eight o'clock the previous evening. She sounded cut up, devastated. It was clear to Jack that the shock of seeing him again had made her react in the way she had, and he forgave her. Of course he did; she was his daughter.

She didn't say much when she got to his place; she'd just wanted to go straight to bed. She seemed exhausted — more worn down than worn out — and Jack had more than enough good sense not to force the issue. As much as he wanted to see Emily as his little girl in pigtails, those days were over. And he hadn't seen nearly half as many of them as he would've liked. Now, she was a teenager. She had her own ideas, her own direction. Her own life.

He'd opened the door to the spare room, just a few inches, around half an hour after she'd closed the door and gone to bed. It didn't seem right having her sleep in her old bedroom. Besides which, he'd long since moved everything of hers into the loft. All that was in there now were boxes and stored furniture.

The first thing that struck him was how different she looked sleeping to how she did when she was awake. He would've said she looked just fine when she was awake, but only seeing the peaceful, serene look on her face as she slept had made him realise the pain and anguish she must be feeling in her waking hours. He wanted more than anything to walk over and cradle her, feel like the protective father. But he knew he couldn't. This had to be done one step at a time.

The miniature clock on the mantelpiece gave one small, tinny gong to signal it was exactly half past nine. He'd been awake for well over twenty-four hours — almost twenty-eight — but he didn't feel tired.

He looked at the glass of whisky on the table next to him, still untouched from last night, and registered the sound of movement upstairs. A few seconds later, he heard the noise of Emily's footsteps on the stairs, getting louder as she made her way down and opened the door to the living room.

Jack looked at her.

'Morning.'

Emily lifted her chin momentarily, as if to acknowledge him without saying a word. Her dark hair was tied back, part of her fringe hanging lank over one cheekbone, a black hoody coming down almost to her knees.

'Bit early for a teenager to be up, isn't it? I was expecting peace and quiet until well after lunch.'

Emily seemed unsure how to respond at first, but eventually gave a half-forced smile.

'What's for breakfast?' she said, pushing the stray bit of fringe back over her ear, the ends of her fingers barely visible past the end of the hoody's long black sleeves.

Her eyes fell on Jack's whisky glass.

His followed.

'That's from last night,' he said. 'I poured it before you texted me. I just haven't thrown it away yet.'

Emily nodded. Jack couldn't tell whether she believed him or not. In any case, what did it matter? Was he not allowed to drink whisky in his own home? Or had Helen and her parents fed Emily stories about Jack being some sort of stereotypical drink-driven detective? He didn't know, and he wasn't sure he wanted to.

'What would you like?' he said. 'I can rustle up a mean scrambled eggs on toast.'

'Sounds good,' she said, without any hint of tone whatsoever.

The eggy mixture cracked and sizzled as he moved it around the pan with a wooden spatula. He was aware of

Emily sitting at his kitchen table behind him, hands wrapped around a mug of milky coffee.

'I hope the milk's still alright. I have mine black, so I don't tend to use it much. Mind you, I've put a splash in the eggs, too, so at least we'll both get it. Good job I've got two bathrooms.'

He turned slightly to look at Emily. She didn't seem to register him speaking at all. Instead, she just looked down into her mug of coffee.

The eggs cooked, Jack spooned them onto two slices of toast and slid one over to her.

He took a mouthful and then asked the question he'd wanted to ask her ever since last night.

'So. What brings you here?'

Emily shrugged, not taking her eyes from the mug. Jack could see her black nail polish was slightly chipped, the nails bitten back as far as they'd go.

'Problems with Nan and Grandad?' he asked.

She shuffled in her chair and let out what sounded like half a sigh.

He took another mouthful of scrambled egg.

'How often do you see your mum?'

Another shrug.

'I must admit, she didn't tell me much about you,' he said. 'I didn't even see her until quite recently, when she knocked at my door. I don't know where she'd been.' He took a sip of coffee. 'Do you remember the house at all?'

Emily shook her head. He felt relieved that he

wouldn't get any backlash for moving all her stuff into the loft.

'Not really,' she said. 'Bits of it. I remember the living room wallpaper. You haven't decorated.'

Jack smiled. 'Does that surprise you?'

She shook her head again.

'I honestly had no idea where you were. All I knew is your mum had left and taken you with her. I heard something on the grapevine later on about Spain. I tried to find you. I even booked a flight out there, but I couldn't find you,' he said, not mentioning the fact that he'd not actually got on the plane. 'Emily, look, I don't know what your mother and your grandparents have said. I know it won't have been nice stuff. I know how things work in the heat of the moment. But I... I just wanted to say thank you. For coming here. For coming to see for yourself that I'm not such a bad bloke after all.'

Emily put her knife and fork on her plate and pushed her chair backwards.

'Can I go now?'

Jack looked down at her breakfast. 'You haven't finished yet. There's still half of it on your plate.'

'I've got places to be,' she said, getting up and walking into the hall. Jack stood and watched her pick up her rucksack, sling it over her shoulder and open the front door.

'Will I see you later?'

'I'll text you,' she said, closing the door behind her.

3

James Aston looked again at the image on his mobile phone. He'd transferred them from his computer before leaving the house, just in case he needed them. He blinked twice, squinting to make sure he was seeing what he thought he was seeing. The images were never of particularly good quality, but that was the way they had to be. Getting any closer would raise suspicions. But as fuzzy and indistinct as the wording itself was, the message was clear.

He'd been waiting to see something like this for a long time: something hard, concrete. Something that could finally blow the lid on everything. Something that could bring his family back to him.

Again, he looked at the photograph. He needed to make sure. He needed to be certain. Sure, some of the letters were difficult to tell apart — was that an A or an E? — but that was all more or less irrelevant. It was obvious what it said. Would anyone else see the same message he was seeing? He didn't know, but he had to take the risk. It was now or never.

Before he could even think about what he was doing, he was striding towards the phone box. A thousand thoughts flooded through his mind. Was this an emergency? Probably not, he thought. After all, there wouldn't be a whole lot they could do right now. The damage had been done. *101*, the non-emergency number, would be the most sensible option. He lifted the handset, then paused for a moment. If what the message had said was real, lives could be at stake. It was down to him to act. He dialled *999*, the emergency number.

A man answered his call. James froze for a moment, unsure of what to say. There was so much he wanted to say, but he had to keep it brief and to the point. Anything else, and they'd think he was a crackpot. No-one in their right mind would believe the whole story, not at first. Not even the police.

'Hello, police emergency.' the voice at the other end of the phone said.

'Uh, yes,' James replied, eventually. 'Hi. Uh, there's a dead body. Someone's been murdered.'

4

Wendy curled a nostril in disgust at the state of the coffee mugs, and rifled through the cupboard to try and find one that could pass as almost clean. She needed to get another one of her own, with her name plastered over it. The last one had gone walkabout, as did everything else in the office sooner or later, and she hadn't got round to replacing it yet.

Eventually, she found one that didn't look too bad. She ran the hot tap until it was scalding, squirted a good quarter of a cup of washing-up liquid into the mug and scrubbed at it with a handful of scrunched-up paper towels. She rinsed it with the boiling water and sat it in the sink for a minute or so, hoping the steaming liquid would kill off the rest of the germs lurking in the porcelain.

The major incident room was quieter than usual — even quieter than it would usually be following the closure of any large case — and Wendy put this down to Jack Culverhouse's absence. She didn't know if he'd booked a holiday. She doubted it. But then again she tried to block out a lot of what he said. It wasn't that she disrespected her boss; she just needed to try and keep her sanity occasionally.

'Righto,' Steve Wing said into the phone, raising his hand to stop Wendy as she walked past. 'I'll pass it on. Cheers. Bye.'

Wendy looked at Steve, waiting for him to tell her what he wanted.

'A report of a body,' he said. 'The caller reckons it's a murder.'

'Good job we don't need to pay pathologists, isn't it?' Wendy joked. 'What did they discover at the scene?'

'Uh, nothing,' Steve replied.

'What do you mean *nothing*?'

'Nothing. The first responders can't get in. They're calling for backup.'

'What, backup from CID?' Wendy said, raising her voice.

'Well, no, uniform are waiting for more of their own, but there's only one reason the owners would deny access, isn't there? If they're trying to hide evidence or whatever, we'll need CID on the scene sharpish.'

Wendy narrowed her eyes. 'Are you serious? What if it's a hoax? Uniform just want to call CID out on a whim?' She considered how lucky Steve was that Culverhouse wasn't around to have this conversation with him. 'Where is it, anyway?'

'That's the thing,' Steve replied. 'It's at Hilltop Farm.'

The name rang a bell. Most local people knew of Hilltop Farm. There were stories about it being some sort of hippy commune or home to a religious group. But the farm had never fallen across the police's radar, as far as Wendy knew. It was just another idiosyncrasy that made up the quirky fabric of the Mildenheath area.

'And they're denying access?' Wendy asked.

'Yep. Something about only allowing people in if they're part of the Kingdom of God. The first responders said they're allowed to enter private land if they believe someone's committed a crime. Their response was that it's not private land; it's God's land.'

Wendy sighed. 'Sounds like fun. Get the DCI on the phone and tell him. He'll make a call on it.'

'Tried that,' Steve replied. 'Got no reply, so I sent a text.'

Wendy shook her head. She was often tempted to make a move away from Mildenheath and join a police force that operated in the same way as the rest of the country. Policing in Mildenheath was often a law unto itself. That was something that was changing, but not quickly enough for Wendy's liking. That a Detective Chief Inspector could just ignore phone calls and not turn up for work would be unthinkable elsewhere. Proper procedures would have to be put in place, rules followed. But not here. She'd had something of a change of heart in recent months, wondering if perhaps Jack Culverhouse wasn't such a bad bloke after all. That was quickly starting to change again.

'Looks like you're in charge for the moment,' Steve added.

'Me? I'm a DS, Steve. The same as you.'

'Yeah, but you're more... Well, you're more senior. In a way, I mean.'

'More senior?' Wendy asked. 'Is that meant to mean old?'

'Well no, obviously not,' Steve replied, adding that he was well aware he had a good few years on her. 'But you're kind of his right-hand woman, aren't you? His second-in-command.'

Wendy raised her eyebrows. 'Steve, if this is your way of getting out of making decisions, you can stick it up your arse. If you want us to attend the scene, we can attend the scene. But I'll be buggered if I'm going to be the one to make that decision.'

Steve looked at her and smiled. She knew exactly what he was thinking. Never mind being Jack Culverhouse's right-hand woman; she was starting to become him.

5

Wendy spotted Jack Culverhouse's car parked up on a grass verge as she pulled up behind it on the rural track known as Wellfield Lane. Culverhouse got out of his car at the same time as Wendy and Steve, the two of them both surprised to see the DCI in attendance.

'Didn't expect to see you here,' Wendy said, trying to gauge his mood.

'You know me, Knight. Never one to pass up a chance for some hippy bashing. Any sign of the bosher?' he called to the two uniformed officers at the main entrance gate to Hilltop Farm.

'No, sir. But it shouldn't be long.'

The bosher, or Enforcer, was the colloquial police term for the piece of equipment better known as a battering ram. Culverhouse looked up at the wrought iron gates that led into a small walled courtyard. The court-yard had a huge wooden gate behind it. Culverhouse wondered what good the bosher would do in this instance.

'You tried this?' Culverhouse asked, pointing to the intercom box on the wall.

'Yes, of course,' the young uniformed officer replied.

Culverhouse jabbed the button on the box. 'Police. Open up,' he barked.

'I'm sorry, but this is not a public area,' came the muffled and distant reply. 'Please vacate the driveway.'

'Sorry, no can do. We've had a report of a crime and we need to enter the farm.'

The tinny voice returned over the intercom. 'This farm is the land of Christ. No-one has committed a crime here. We are people of God.'

Culverhouse leaned forward and spoke into the intercom. 'I couldn't give a rat's arse if you've got Noah and St Peter in there doing the fucking can-can. We've got two ways of coming in, and one of them means you're going to need to get a new gate. Do I make myself clear?'

There was silence for a few moments.

'Perfectly,' came the eventual reply. 'Someone will be with you in a few moments.'

It took longer than Culverhouse would have liked for someone from the farm to make their way to the front gates. The high walls made it impossible to see inside the farm. It looked more like a prison than a working place of agriculture.

One thing was for sure, though: It was huge. The wall seemed to go on forever, and Wendy considered what they might find behind the gates. Should they have called for even more backup? She could see now why the two uniformed officers felt a little out of their depth when they first arrived. But further backup needed to come from around twenty miles away. It would be some time before they'd have any more strength in numbers.

Going into a place like this was always a risk. Most police officers would put their lives on the line most days. Granted, the same couldn't really be said of CID. But, once again, Mildenheath was different. Here, plain-clothes detectives did a lot of the legwork, as opposed to uniformed officers. Mildenheath and the surrounding area had a high level of crime in general. With the government slashing policing budgets left, right and centre, a different approach was often needed just to cope.

But that wasn't the biggest concern at the forefront of anyone's minds as they waited for someone to open up the farm. The largest worry was that someone could be hiding or destroying evidence during the ensuing delay. That could jeopardise any future investigation, and was one of the main reasons for searching the property as quickly as possible.

When the solid wooden gate opened, a large man appeared. He seemed to be of African origin, and looked to Jack and Wendy more like a bouncer than a vicar. They watched him as he walked through the first gate and went to open the wrought iron ones at the front of the farm. Culverhouse leaned forward to get a better look. The man's hand disappeared from view for a moment, and seemed to be fiddling with the wall.

'Don't worry,' the man said. 'I'm turning a key. The gate's locked with electromagnets.'

'Electromagnets? On a church?' Culverhouse asked.

'It's not a church,' the man replied, offering no further information as he opened the gate and stood aside.

'Whatever it is, don't you think it's overkill? That sort of security tends to make us think people are hiding something.'

The man just smiled.

'Where are we meant to be going?' Culverhouse said aside to one of the uniformed officers.

'The old grain store, apparently,' came the reply.

'It's over there, to the right of the white building,' the man said. 'Let me know if you need anything else.'

There was something in his tone that told Wendy they were being set up for a fall. Whatever evidence there was — if any — would have been hidden or destroyed by now. There was no other reason why the man would be so helpful all of a sudden. She'd almost discounted the possibility of an ambush. Almost. The small chance was something that played on her mind as she walked a couple of paces behind Jack Culverhouse, toward the grain store.

What struck Wendy most was that there seemed to be no-one else around. There were many buildings scattered around the vast farm, but no people. The only people she could see were her own team and the man who'd opened the gates and was now leading them towards the large, looming grain store. The whole place just felt spooky and wrong, somehow.

It was clear that no-one had used the building for storing grain for quite some time. At least, that's what Wendy hoped. The missing tiles on the curved roof and the white paint flaking off the exterior walls gave the grain store a feeling of neglect. Indeed, the whole farm seemed to feel somewhat forgotten and abandoned in some ways, but fresh and invigorating in others. She supposed that was one of the hallmarks of a community locked away from the outside world.

The door creaked as the man unlatched it and swung it open, that being the only sound save for the officers' own blood thumping in their ears. Wendy swallowed as her eyes adjusted to the darkness and she tried to take in the sight in front of her.

6

Ben Gallagher scratched at his beard and stared through the gap in the curtains, watching the unfolding scene at the grain store. He knew exactly what the police would find there, and he knew it would make no immediate difference. But that was the whole point. It would plant a seed in their minds. It would open a paper trail. And there might well be something they'd spot while they were here — something which could start to unravel the whole operation.

He hadn't expected them to spring into action so quickly. He couldn't even be certain his messages were getting out — until now. That was a good thing, though. If he couldn't be sure his messages were getting to their intended target, there was little chance of Father Kümmel or his henchmen finding anything out.

Father Kümmel must have believed he was pretty

secure. Hilltop Farm had been shut off from the outside world for as long as Ben could remember — long before he'd arrived here, anyway. Save for very few trusted members, referred to as missionaries, nobody got out. Sometimes new people came in, but that was increasingly rare. Ben often wondered why that was.

It was the missionaries' job to recruit new members, to convert people to the faith. And they sold the story well. Ben's own father had brought himself, Ben and Ben's brother, Harry, to Hilltop Farm almost twenty-five years earlier. The church preached self-reliance, community cohesion and protection from the outside world. They warned of the evils that existed and were growing within the world — corporate domination, an over-reliance on money, untold government corruption — all noble causes, but Ben knew this was just a smokescreen.

His own father had come to Hilltop Farm in the early nineties. There'd been a recession under the Conservative government which caused his and many other small businesses to fold. The same government's previous recession in the early 80s had cost him his well-paid job then. He was a prime target for Kümmel's church. The idea of self-reliance and freedom from money and corruption was an attractive one. After his wife, Ben's mother, had taken the opportunity to run off with another man, his mind was made up.

Ben was three years old. Since then, the church and Hilltop Farm had been all he'd ever known. He'd grown up here, made friends here, had dedicated his young life to the church. But as he grew older he had started to doubt.

Harry was six years older than he was. He'd been nine years old when their father had brought them to Hilltop Farm. Harry had known life on the outside, life in the wider world. It wasn't something he ever spoke openly about. Most people on the farm suspected what would happen to them if they expressed any interest to leave. But there were occasions when Ben had picked up on things Harry had said or done, little looks he gave.

And then, one day, he was gone.

Ben could still remember waking up that morning, well over three years ago now, unable to find his brother. In the coming days and weeks, the church wardens and overseers told Ben and his father they didn't know what had happened to Harry. The unspoken truth was that Harry had escaped. But that was something the church leaders would never address or acknowledge. Father Kümmel always told the apostles that they were free to leave at any time, but no-one in the church knew of anyone who had successfully done so. Ben's father became convinced that Harry had rejected God, and God had punished him for his sins. He said he'd been taken in the night into the Kingdom of God to atone for his lack of faith.

Ben felt comforted in the belief that Harry had escaped back to the outside world, but worried that Father Kümmel's missionaries might not be as benevolent as they made themselves out to be. He had nightmares of them tracking Harry down and bringing him back to Hilltop Farm — or worse.

Until one morning, when he'd truly received a message from above.

7

The inside of the grain store looked as uncared-for and dilapidated as Wendy had expected. The structure was still there, but she could see the sunlight streaming in through the missing roof tiles, the wooden beams and panelling stained with damp patches where the water had got in. The inside of the building looked as open to the elements as the outside. No-one had stored grain in here for some time. There were no interior rooms, no hiding holes, no corners. They were surrounded purely by stone, damp patches and the odd hole in the roof.

She took one of the first response officers to one side while Culverhouse spoke to the man who'd led them here.

'What else did the call say?' she asked.

'That there was a body in the grain store,' the officer replied. 'The body of a woman.'

'Did they give any more detail? Like who the woman was?'

'No, not that I know of,' he said. 'It was pretty brief, apparently.'

Wendy stepped back outside into the light, took out her phone and called the control centre. She looked up at the sky. It was threatening to rain. The last thing she wanted was for more water to seep into the grain store and destroy any potential evidence that was in there — if there was any.

'I'm at Hilltop Farm,' she whispered, once she'd managed to get through to someone who could help her. 'This call that came in about a body. Can you tell me a bit more about it?'

The controller took a moment to retrieve the details. 'Yeah, pretty short call. Nineteen seconds in total. Mostly just him repeating himself. He seemed pretty agitated, so we took it seriously.'

'Where did he call from? Did he leave any details?' Wendy asked.

'No details. Call came from a phone box in Milden-heath. Allerdale Road, it says here.'

Wendy sighed. She'd known of anonymous calls made from that box before, and recalled that it wasn't covered by CCTV. She doubted that was a situation which had since been rectified. Very few things in Mildenheath ever got fixed or improved. She thanked the controller, ended the call and put her phone back in her pocket.

She stepped back inside the building.

'Is this the only grain store on the farm?' she asked.

'Yes,' came the man's terse reply.

'You obviously don't store grain in here, though. And I presume you don't pop out to get your bread from Tesco, so where do you store grain now?'

'Kitchens.'

Wendy sensed she wasn't going to get much out of him.

'What's your name?' Culverhouse asked.

The man turned and looked at him for a moment, no expression on his face.

'Nelson.'

'And what's your role here?'

Nelson smiled. 'I help to look after the farm.'

'Funny. You don't look like a farmer,' Culverhouse said.

'"For the Lord sees not as man sees: man looks on the outward appearance, but the Lord looks on the heart." Samuel, chapter sixteen, verse seven.'

It was Culverhouse's turn to smile. 'So in other words you're trying to tell me you're not the big, burly protection racket engineer you look like?'

Wendy placed a hand on his arm. 'Guv, I think we should—'

'I am a spiritual man, Detective Chief Inspector,' the man said, interrupting. 'I serve my God and I help Father Kümmel to look after our apostles. We are a close community, bound by God.' By the time he reached the end of his sentence, Nelson was almost toe-to-toe with Culverhouse, towering a good eight to ten inches over him.

'Right. Well I'm glad we got that sorted,' Culverhouse

said, stepping backwards and heading towards the entrance to the grain store. 'Mind if we speak to this Father Kümmel?'

Nelson shrugged. 'I can ask him.'

As they entered what Nelson had referred to as the chapel, Wendy wondered whether this farm was connected to the electricity grid at all. This building, like the old grain store, suffered from a distinct lack of light. The windows — if, indeed, that's what they were — were not only tiny, but high up on the walls. It reminded Wendy more of a prison cell than a chapel. The whole building smelt damp and musty. It was grim enough at this time of year, but she wondered what it would be like here in the depths of a particularly harsh winter.

Father Joseph Kümmel sat at an ornate wooden desk, which looked entirely out of place in this building. Wendy doubted very much whether it was permanently situated here. She didn't suppose it would last five minutes with this amount of damp in the air. All for show, she thought.

'Father, this lady and gentleman are from the police,' Nelson told him. DS Steve Wing had accompanied the uniformed officers in a more detailed search of the old grain store, watched over by another of the church's heavies.

'The police?' he replied, with a voice of calm surprise. 'How unusual. I don't recall us having been visited by the police before. How can I be of assistance?'

Wendy had assumed from the off that he would have been well aware of their presence. There was no way they would have opened the gates and let the police in without word from the very top. Hilltop Farm had been a closed community for decades, and she was pretty sure that hadn't just changed this morning.

'We received a call earlier today alerting us to the possibility of a death here on the farm,' Culverhouse said, jumping in before Wendy had a chance to speak.

'A death?' the pastor said, placing a hand over his heart. 'I do hope not. Have you heard anything about anyone dying, Nelson?'

'No, Father Joseph. Nothing,' Nelson replied.

'Do you have any information on who it is who's supposed to have died?' he asked, addressing Culverhouse.

Wendy looked at her boss. They could both see exactly where this was going.

'No, we don't have an identity,' Wendy said, trying to assist the DCI.

The pastor's face relaxed. 'I see. I think I know exactly what this is,' he said, standing and pacing the room. 'You do realise that this is not a church in the conventional sense, Detective Sergeant? We are a closed community church. That means the traditional churches see us as pretenders and the wider community sees us as wackos and nut-jobs. We try to live a peaceful existence here. We are self-sufficient and we have no reliance on the outside world or the greater economy. Of course, that does not sit comfortably with many people.'

'Are you saying this was a hoax call?' Culverhouse asked.

'I'm saying, Detective Chief Inspector, that you have gained access to the church's property, discovered that there is no dead body and seen for yourself that we are a peaceful and harmless people. The rest, I am sure, you can deduce for yourself.'

'I think you'll find we *finally* gained access to the church's property after threatening to smash the gates in, have only searched one building on the farm so far and the only people we've seen have been you and two of your goons.'

The pastor smiled. 'On the contrary, you were informed that Hilltop Farm was private property, and you are perfectly welcome to dig wherever you like and speak to whomever you please. You can even help with the harvest, if you like. Kill two birds with one stone. I'll lend you my own shovel.'

Culverhouse nodded, holding eye contact with the pastor. 'We'll be in touch.'

'Shouldn't we do a more thorough search?' Wendy asked Culverhouse as he strode towards his car. 'I mean, I know it's a tricky one to call, but something's not quite right, don't you think?'

'Thinking's dangerous, Knight. I prefer to look at the facts in front of us. And let's face it — there aren't any.'

'You're still not answering me,' Wendy said, standing

between him and his driver's door. 'Something's not right, and you know it. What about the way he referred to us both by our ranks? How the hell did he know what rank we were? We never even introduced ourselves to him.'

'So he's seen our pictures in the Mildenheath Gazette a couple of times. And what?'

'Are you serious? A religious cult, cut off from the outside world for decades, but still has the local paper delivered?' Wendy said, with a derisive snort.

'Oh yes, you're totally right,' Culverhouse replied. 'It's completely unlike churches and religious groups to be hypocritical, isn't it?' He could see Wendy wasn't budging. He sighed. 'Look, what do you want me to do? I can't go sending in a team of fucking JCBs to dig up a farm just because some crackpot made an anonymous call from a phone box to say there's a dead body somewhere. And who do you suppose made the call, by the way, considering no-one gets in or out of Hilltop Farm?'

Wendy had to admit that she didn't have a response to that. She was convinced there was something far more than met the eye. But she also knew she was going to have to go some — not for the first time — to convince her boss.

8

Ben stood as still as he could, his feet planted on the floor as he watched Father Joseph Kümmel begin to speak. The atmosphere was tense to say the least; an air of expectant anticipation filled the air. It wasn't often that Father Joseph assembled everyone in the community in one place to speak to them directly. The fact that he was doing it out here in the open courtyard seemed symbolic to Ben. *Let's get everything out in the open.* The low, late afternoon sun was making him squint, and accentuating his headache.

Father Joseph liked to maintain an aura of elusiveness where possible. Where necessary, his sermons aside, he'd be seen but not heard. If he summoned you to the chapel, you knew it was important. Your heart would be thumping in your chest. You knew you were going to come face to face with him, fortunate enough to be able to share a room with him alone. It was always a huge moment, and it'd fill you with awe, respect and a small amount of fear.

Not fear in a bad way; more a fear of disappointing him. That was the sort of power he held over people. Thinking back and looking at things objectively, Ben could see that Father Joseph was a master of manipulation. He gave people everything they desired at that moment in time: protection from the outside world, food, comfort and relative warmth. They felt safe, or at least safer than they did on the outside.

As Father Joseph spoke, everyone else was completely silent. His deep voice filled the outdoor space as if they were all packed inside a small room.

'My children, I am sorry to have to report that earlier today I was made aware of an attempt by someone on the outside to besmirch the good name of our church. As you are all aware, belonging to the church is a matter of free will. Anyone is free to leave at any time. You need only come and ask me.'

Ben could see a few heads nodding.

'As most of you have been members of the church for a good many years, you all know the way of life that we are able to enjoy here. Because we are able to enjoy that way of life, dark forces on the outside want to do us harm. Of course, I would never say that those who have left or doubted their faith are in any way responsible for this. But I think we should all pray for their souls, and that they might find the way to ensuring a gracious respect to the community that gave them so much.'

The crowd began to murmur their agreement and

lowered their head in prayer. A minute or so later, Father Joseph spoke again.

'And if any members of the church should have any worries or concerns whatsoever, you all know that you can speak with me. You are all welcome to the chapel at any time.'

Ben tried to hold a straight face. He knew damn well that direct access to Father Joseph was kept limited. He also knew that no-one would even dare to try and impose on Father Joseph's time for anything any less trivial than imminent death. He had cultivated the perfect cult of personality: making himself seem at the same time both approachable and omnipotent.

As Father Joseph spoke, Ben heard the sound of an approaching helicopter. It wasn't a rare sound to hear on the farm, particularly as it was on the flight path between two Royal Air Force bases. But on this particular occasion it chilled him to the bone. It wasn't the sound itself. It was the fact that Father Joseph had stopped speaking and was looking up to the sky, watching the helicopter pass over-head. Ben didn't know if it was his own guilty conscience speaking, but he could swear he saw the early stages of paranoia crossing Father Joseph's mind.

9

The day had been a washout, as far as Jack Culverhouse was concerned. It had started late, as it was. The visit to Hilltop Farm had been less than successful, and he'd spent the rest of the afternoon writing up more sodding paperwork. He estimated that for every hour spent doing some actual work, he'd spend another two writing reports about it. It was one of the things that wound him up about modern policing. To him, paperwork and filing were for office managers and secretaries; police officers did policing.

The job had become increasingly bureaucratic over the years. The fairly recent introduction of politically elected Police and Crime Commissioners had almost tipped him over the edge. Not only was he answerable to red tape and desk-bound management, but he now had politicians breathing down his neck. And not just any old politician, either: Martin Cummings, the sort of man who assumes a position way beyond his capabilities and makes up for it by enacting swingeing changes just for the sake of it. Still, Cummings was up for re-election shortly, and Culver-house would be the first person waiting outside the polling station that morning with pen in hand.

For now, though, he was taking every day as it came. He knew he had a cushy number compared to most people in his position. CID departments were being merged all over the place, and the rest of the county had been moved into Milton House, the purpose-built county police HQ more than twenty miles away. An office block. Milden-heath Police Station, at barely forty years old, was hardly a beautiful old building but at least it was a police station. A proper nick. It had cold brick walls, broken radiators and a fucking awful canteen. But at least it wasn't all glass partitions, swipe-card entry and lifts.

He'd finally chucked last night's whisky down the sink before he left to head to Hilltop Farm earlier, and he had half considered pouring himself another one when he got home, but he realised that would've just been habit. When he thought about it, he didn't actually want one. He didn't know what he wanted, other than to put some utter crap on the telly and zone out for a bit. A couple of hours to not think about dead bodies, bureaucracy and trying to kick water uphill. 'All part of the fun,' Detective Sergeant Frank Vine would say. It wound Jack up that Frank was such a cantankerous old bastard but could always manage to come out with some sort of motivational witticism whenever anyone else dared to have a bad day.

Just as he was starting to zone out in front of a travel

documentary, he heard the front door open. He'd given Emily a key. She was the only person he trusted with one, despite the fact that he'd not seen her in nine years and had no idea how trustworthy she was now. But then again, if you couldn't trust your own children, who could you trust?

He heard her rucksack thud on the floor before she walked through into the living room.

'Nice day?' he asked, trying to be as normal and relaxed as possible.

'Was alright,' she replied, heading straight for the kitchen.

'I was thinking about what we'll do when you go back to school,' he called after her, not moving from his seat on the sofa. 'You've only got a few days left before you go back. I mean, I'm happy to try and sort out timings with work and drive you up there each morning and pick you up, if you wanted to stay here occasionally. Only I don't think there's a direct bus from here. Or perhaps... Well, I don't know,' he said, leaving that out in the open. He wasn't about to suggest out loud that Emily transfer to a school in Mildenheath. He didn't even know how long she would be staying with him. Hell, he didn't even know why she'd turned up in the first place, but he certainly wasn't going to ask her to go anywhere. He was enjoying having her around, or at least knowing that she was nearby and safe. They were both things he hadn't been able to enjoy knowing for the past nine years.

For now, he was just going to ride with it and pretend everything was as normal as possible. He got the impression from Emily that was what she wanted. She'd had more than enough drama and upheaval. They both had.

'Milk's off,' she said, holding the carton out through the doorway so he could see it.

'Seriously? It was alright this morning,' Jack replied.

'Well it's off now,' came the response, followed by the sound of her pouring it down the sink.

Jack cursed his luck. He'd managed to miss the good years — seeing Emily through school, watching her learn musical instruments, seeing her blossom into a well-rounded child — and he'd instead managed to come in at the tail end and have a stroppy teenager to deal with. He decided to join her in the kitchen. They were going to have a conversation whether she liked it or not.

'Do you want some dinner?' he asked, thinking of making himself a cup of tea but then remembering there was now no milk.

'I've eaten.'

'Where?' He realised he didn't even know where she'd spent the day, never mind where she might have eaten. Should he have made more of a point of asking her before she left this morning? Or should he be asking her now? Or would both of those options put him in the bracket of 'over-bearing parent'? He didn't know; he hadn't been here before. There wasn't much call for that sort of interrogation when she was four. He felt like he'd only been given the first few pages of the instruction manual.

'Out,' Emily replied, giving him absolutely no information whatsoever. That didn't sit right with him. Jack

Culverhouse's world revolved around information. He was keen not to alienate Emily within the first twenty-four hours, but he decided he was still her father and still needed to know where she had been. She wasn't even fourteen, for Christ's sake.

'But where? You've been out the whole day. Do you work?'

Emily raised an eyebrow and curled the corner of her mouth. 'Dad, I'm thirteen. And before you ask, no I didn't fancy a sodding paper round.'

Jack sighed. 'Emily, you have to understand. You're almost... Well, you'll be an adult soon. I'm trying to work out what's gone on, what's going on. I've been wondering where you were for the past nine years, and now you're just... Look, can you at least let me know what's going on? Where we stand? Don't get me wrong, I love having you here and I'm really pleased that you've dropped by, but—'

'Dropped by?' Emily said, raising her voice and interrupting him. 'Dropped by? Seriously? Like, I was just passing and wanted to say hi and pop in for a cuppa? Really?'

'No, that's not what I mean,' Jack replied, desperate to explain. 'What I mean is—'

'Yeah yeah, I know what you mean.'

Jack shook his head. 'No. No, you don't. I'm trying, Emily. I'm trying to verbalise something that can't be put into words. All I want to know is where I stand.'

'Where you stand? Jesus Christ, you're my dad. What do you mean you don't know where you stand?'

'Well how long are you staying here? Is this going to be a regular thing? Listen, I love having you around, but I'd just like to know what your plans are. Is that too much to ask?'

Emily stared at him for a few minutes, a disgusted look on her face, before she shook her head and turned to open the fridge door. As she did so, Jack noticed a mark on her neck, poking out under her hoodie, visible just for a fleeting moment as she turned her head.

'What's that?' he asked, trying to remain as calm as possible, even though he knew damn well what it was.

'What?'

'On your neck.'

'Nothing,' Emily replied, pulling her hoodie further round her neck.

'Don't give me nothing, Emily. It's a love bite.'

'It's a rash.'

'It's a love bite. I know a fucking love bite when I see one.'

Emily said nothing for a few moments, and seemed to be staring into the fridge. She turned and looked at him.

'And so what if it is? What are you going to do about it?'

Jack had been thrown a curveball. 'What am I going to do about it? What do you mean? What do you want me to do about it?'

Emily shook her head. Another look of disappointed disgust.

'What's his name?' he asked as she started to turn back towards the fridge.

'Who?'

'Don't start playing games, Em. Who gave you the love bite?'

'Duh, my boyfriend?' she replied, phrasing it more like a question than a statement and putting on a mock-dumb voice.

Jack could feel the tension rising up inside himself. Emily wasn't old enough for boyfriends. She was thirteen years old. Who was he? How old was he? What did they get up to? In his mind, Emily was still barely out of nappies. This didn't seem right, didn't feel right.

'What's his name?'

Jack thought for a moment she wasn't going to answer him. It took her a second or two to consider it, but finally she told him.

'Ethan.'

'Ethan what?' he asked, almost immediately.

'What, so you can go looking on your little police computer to see what you can find out about him you mean? You're so transparent, Dad.' She moved to leave the kitchen and walk back through to the living room, but Jack stepped to the side and stood in her way.

'Oh, so he'll be on it will he?'

'Don't be stupid.'

'I'm not being stupid, Emily, by wanting to know the name of my daughter's boyfriend.'

She crossed her arms and shook her head again. 'You're

unreal, you are. You don't show up for nine years, and when you finally crawl out of the woodwork you suddenly want to interrogate me about my private life. What gives you the right?'

Jack clenched his teeth and tried not to explode. He chose to ignore the first part of her comment. 'I'm not interrogating you. I'm just asking you what his name is.'

'I told you,' she replied. 'Ethan.'

'His surname, I mean.'

'Why? You want to look him up, don't you?'

Jack sighed. 'No. I'm not going to look him up.'

Emily looked at him. He could see her eyes moving between each of his, trying to suss him out.

'Turner. Ethan Turner. Happy?'

10

Jack had slept soundly for the first time in a long time. He and Emily had sat and watched TV all evening. They barely said a word to each other, but that didn't bother him. He was just pleased to have her there, and she didn't seem to mind too much either.

He'd asked her whether her grandparents knew where she was. She said they did. She added that they weren't particularly happy about it, but they understood. He knew he was going to have to call them and explain the situation from his point of view. He'd have to make sure she had her belongings and her schooling sorted, especially if she was going to be staying with him during school time. But right now he was still struggling to come to terms with what was happening.

In his mind, he supposed it was probably fairly normal for her to just rock up somewhere and dump herself. After all, she'd been shoved from pillar to post already. Her mum had taken her from her family home and left her with the grandparents while she swanned off to God knows where.

When he'd got up that morning, he was surprised to see Emily was already up and about. She'd been downstairs, got herself a bowl of cereal (without milk) and was listening to the radio. She'd told him she was going back to her grandparents'. His face had dropped, but he tried not to show it. When she said she'd be back later, he smiled. There was still a hell of a lot to sort out, but the signs were all positive.

Once he'd got to work, though, things were feeling far less positive. There was a note on his voicemail asking him to report to the Chief Constable when he got in. Charles Hawes, the current Chief Constable, was technically based at county headquarters in Milton House, but chose to keep an office at Mildenheath for much the same reasons as Jack Culverhouse wanted to keep away from HQ. It was a handy thing to sell to the public, too. The head of the county's police force had chosen not to sit in a plush office in the countryside, but was instead positioned right in the nerve centre of CID and community policing in one of the most police-dependent parts of the county. Then again, spin was half the game.

Hawes had been threatening to retire for years. He'd even announced it to Jack a few months back, but since then things had gone quiet on that front. Charles Hawes wasn't the retiring type. They'd be dragging him out of here in a box.

Jack knew exactly what Hawes wanted. He'd have

heard about the shenanigans at Hilltop Farm the previous day and would want answers. Hawes always wanted answers. Not for himself — he trusted Jack Culverhouse more or less implicitly — but for the Police and Crime Commissioner, Martin Cummings. Hawes was the last of the old guard. He wasn't quite as old school as Jack, but he nonetheless respected the DCI's ways and let him get away with far more than he deserved at times. Cummings had been keen for Hawes to retire for some time. Jack supposed that was why Hawes had never gone through with it, secretly hoping that he'd last longer than the PCC's electoral term and be able to leave on his own terms, rather than being pushed out by some sleazy no-mark politician.

But all Cummings was worried about were the column inches. It wouldn't look good for the force to either be too heavy handed — particularly where religion was involved — nor would it be ideal, to say the least, for them to have been seen to have neglected their duties if there were serious suspicions of a crime being reported at Hilltop Farm.

Regardless, Jack made his way to the Chief Constable's office and prepared to waste half an hour on a lecture he could already reel off word for word before he even got there.

Hawes smiled as Culverhouse entered, as he always did, and beckoned for him to sit down. The office was as smart as it could be in this dreary old 1970s building, but Jack liked it. It had a certain style.

'I suppose you can guess why I've asked you to come and see me, Jack,' the Chief Constable said.

Culverhouse raised both eyebrows for a moment. He wasn't going to need three guesses.

'Hilltop Farm,' he replied.

'Indeed. Can you run me through what happened?'

Culverhouse took a deep breath. 'We received a call yesterday morning from someone reporting a death on the farm. We—'

'Who received the call?' Hawes asked.

'Who on our team, you mean? DS Wing, I think, sir.'

'You think? Were you not there?'

Culverhouse tried to let no emotion show on his face. Did the Chief Constable already know Culverhouse wasn't in the office at the time? Was this all some sort of ruse to make him admit that he'd been sitting at home when he should've been at work as the duty Senior Investigating Officer? He decided to try and keep his language as professional as possible.

'Not at that time, sir. I was late yesterday morning. I'm afraid it couldn't be avoided. Personal circumstances.'

Hawes looked at him and nodded. He knew better than to probe into Jack Culverhouse's private life right now.

'And you heard about the call how?'

'By text message. I met DS Wing and DS Knight at the farm. Uniformed first response officers were already there. They hadn't entered the property due to the reinforced gates and the fact that the residents on the farm would not grant access. They were waiting for backup units to arrive to force entry. I managed to negotiate entry with the residents of the farm.'

'Negotiate?' Hawes asked, raising his eyebrows. The unspoken words were that it wasn't like Jack Culverhouse to *negotiate*.

'Yes, sir. I told them backup units were on their way and we'd be on the property within minutes whether they liked it or not. Subsequently, they let us in.'

'And what did you find?' Hawes asked, sitting back in his chair and interlacing his fingers.

'Not much, to be honest. The call said the body was in the old grain store, but when we got there we could find no sign of it.'

'And what about forensics? Were swabs taken?'

'No, sir. To be perfectly honest, it was a musty, damp old grain store which probably had traces of all sorts of things. I decided that short of bringing in dozens of officers to search the entire farm, which is of considerable size, we had to treat the call as a false alarm. Especially considering the circumstances of the call.'

'Which were?'

'That the caller phoned in anonymously from a phone box in Mildenheath, that whoever called in presumably had little or no inside knowledge of the farm considering it's a completely sealed religious community with no-one going in or out, and that no body could be found.'

The Chief Constable narrowed his eyes. 'Are we sure that no-one goes in or out?'

'I think so, sir. That's what we were told.'

'We're told all sorts of things, Jack. We're the police. It doesn't make those things accurate. But listen. This isn't going to be good for us either way. We've already received a complaint from the church leaders about what they called a raid, and we've also got the possibility that there's been a murder on that farm and we've done nothing about it.'

Culverhouse clenched his teeth. Whatever he'd done, he would've been fucked. And things weren't going to get any easier from here, either. He was simultaneously being roasted for both being too heavy handed and not heavy handed enough. He couldn't win.

'It's a difficult situation, sir. One that needed handling delicately.'

'Father Joseph Kümmel doesn't think it's been handled particularly delicately, Jack.'

'No, he wouldn't,' Jack replied, quickly losing his sense of professionalism. 'But between you and me he's mental. But in my professional opinion the call was a hoax. I imagine the church has made enemies and that there are people who want to drag its name through the mud.'

'Not like you to defend a religious institution, Jack,' the Chief Constable said.

'I'm not defending it. They're a bunch of losers, crack-pots and weirdos. But that doesn't make them murderers.'

Hawes nodded, and took a sip from his glass of water.

'I'm afraid not everyone agrees. There are officers who

have graver concerns about Hilltop Farm and feel it needs investigating further. I'll be honest: I agree with them.'

'Which officers, sir?' Culverhouse asked, knowing damn well who it'd be.

'It's not for me to name names. And anyway, like I said, I agree with them. You don't have any major cases ongoing at the moment, do you? So I think it would be prudent to find out as much as we can about Hilltop Farm and the church that's based there and to make sure our arses are covered. Put it this way — I'd far rather be hauled up for being too heavy handed and digging up the whole fucking farm and finding nothing than I would having to explain that we'd had a murder reported and not investigated it.'

Culverhouse didn't reply.

'Who've you got in at the moment, Jack?' Hawes asked.

'Myself, DS Wing and DS Knight, sir. Frank Vine, Debbie Weston and Ryan Mackenzie are off shift.'

It was yet another quirk of the local policing setup that the town's CID office could run for days on end with just three officers. Then again, it was remarkable that Milden-heath still had a CID office at all. Fortunately, the amount of serious crime was just enough to keep them all in a job, but without being overloaded — except when a huge case threatened to swamp them, as had almost happened once or twice in the past.

'Right. Well I want you to get them all back in,' Hawes said. 'As far as I'm concerned this is now an active investigation.'

11

One of the benefits of being a Detective Chief Inspector was that it was one of the only jobs in which you could phone members of your team on their days off and have them in the office within two hours. That's not to say that any of them were particularly happy, but at least they were there.

Detective Sergeant Frank Vine had, predictably, whinged and whined about it. He was starting to approach the tail end of his career and had made a few noises to Culverhouse about retirement. Generally speaking, the DCI agreed this would probably be a good idea. But then life kept throwing them curveballs. Luke Baxter, a Constable, was killed in the line of duty. Ryan Mackenzie, considered to be his replacement, had joined the team very recently.

Ryan had certainly turned heads on joining Milden-heath CID. Culverhouse hadn't been keen on hearing that a new officer was joining the team part-way through an investigation. He was even less impressed when he found out that Ryan was actually a woman. By the time he'd just about come to terms with that, Ryan had revealed that she was a vegan and was in a lesbian relationship. Neither of those facts would have even registered with most other people. To Jack Culverhouse, it was tantamount to telling him she had three legs.

The final member of the team, Detective Constable Debbie Weston, had long been the silent engine that kept Mildenheath CID running. She never complained, always got on with the job, and was the consummate professional. How she'd been passed over for promotion to Detective Sergeant was beyond Wendy, but she suspected it might have had something to do with the fact that she was a woman.

Culverhouse had briefed the team and recapped what had happened at Hilltop Farm the previous day. He'd also passed on the message that the Chief Constable was keen for the farm to be properly investigated, and that he wasn't particularly supportive of the idea himself.

'Right, let's start from the bottom,' he said, knowing full well that his comments would rile more than a couple of members in his team. 'Ryan, can you get some more information on the original call. See if we can get the recording, get that analysed. See if it matches any other calls we've had recently. Then get onto the local shops and businesses and see who's got CCTV. People even have them on the fronts of their houses nowadays, so I should imagine he'll have been picked up somewhere. Take a look at cars on CCTV too. Even if we don't have the exact area covered, there's a chance you might see a car driving in the direction of the phone box a few minutes before the call and driving away from it a few minutes after. That's a lead we can follow.'

Ryan was nodding and scribbling down notes. Wendy sensed that she'd picked up on Culverhouse's derogatory comment about starting from the bottom, but that she had chosen to rise above it. Good on her, Wendy thought.

'Debbie, I need you to find out what you can about Hilltop Farm. Find out when it came into the ownership of the church, who owned it before, who owns it now. Find out whatever you can about it through the official channels. And have a look on Google Earth, too. We should be able to get a decent idea of the layout of the place. Frank, delve into the finances and Father Joseph's background. I presume the church is registered as some sort of charity or something. Even if it isn't, it has to make or spend money somehow. They'll have rates to pay, land to lease, council tax or something like that. Look it all up. There'll be some sort of paper trail, and if we find out they're even 5p short on their tax bill we'll have something to grab onto.'

Wendy noted that Frank didn't look particularly hopeful of finding anything.

'Knight,' Culverhouse said, choosing to use Wendy's surname, as he always did, 'I'm going to need you to put your diplomatic skills to the test. Get onto Father Joseph Kümmel and his cronies and see if you can get a list of the residents at the farm. He won't tell you anything, and I'm sure he'd be well within his legal rights to do so, but it's got to be worth a shot. And after all, I'm told you have a particularly keen nose for these sorts of things.'

Wendy averted her eyes. She knew exactly what he was getting at. He'd worked out that it was she who'd expressed her concerns to the Chief Constable about a lack of action at Hilltop Farm.

'And Steve?' Culverhouse said, addressing DS Wing. 'You can... Just mop the fucking floor or something. I'm going for a coffee.'

12

Wendy wasn't expecting to get much joy out of her request to see Father Joseph Kümmel. She had no way of phoning ahead or contacting them — they didn't have any phone lines, and they certainly weren't hooked up to email. The only option she had left was to drive over there and try and speak to someone.

They hadn't had much luck last time, and Wendy didn't expect to have any better luck this time. She'd requested that someone else come with her, but Culverhouse had said no. She wasn't keen on entering Hilltop Farm single-crewed. She felt sure that there was something far darker and more sinister going on there than met the eye. But it was what it was, and she was going in alone.

When she got to the gate, she pulled up outside and walked over to the intercom buzzer on the wall. She pressed the button and waited for a response. After a few seconds, the buzzing stopped and it sounded as though someone had picked up the call. But no-one spoke.

'Hello?' Wendy said. 'It's Detective Sergeant Wendy Knight from Mildenheath Police. Would it be possible to speak to somebody from the church, please? I'd like to apologise for what happened yesterday.' She hoped they weren't recording this. She wasn't here to apologise for anything, but thought that perhaps that might be a way to ensure that they let her in.

There was a couple of seconds of silence, until she heard a male voice over the intercom.

'Someone will be with you shortly.'

Wendy noted that even their intercom responses sounded sinister. How could anyone want to live with these people under their own free will? She didn't know much about religious cults and sects, but she knew they tended to prey on desperate, vulnerable people, giving them something they needed at that point in their life. Everything else was just incidental. So what if you weren't allowed to leave? So what if you had to cut off all contact from your family? If you'd been homeless and had no friends and family, and this church came along and gave you a second chance — not to mention a home and protection from the outside world — who wouldn't jump at the chance? Being walled in, they wouldn't know the grass was greener on the other side, either. And with every new generation born at the farm, the knowledge of the outside world shrunk and fear of it grew ever greater.

A couple of minutes later, Wendy heard someone unlocking the inner wooden gate, before it swung open to reveal the man they knew only as Nelson. Nelson opened the iron gates at the front of the complex and stood aside to let her in.

'Father Joseph is in the chapel. Follow me,' he said, locking the gates behind him.

They arrived at what was referred to as the chapel, but in reality was just a damp farmhouse. Wendy was surprised to see that Nelson didn't seem to be going anywhere. He stood near the door, watching her as she spoke to Father Joseph Kümmel.

'We met yesterday,' Wendy said, trying to break the ice.

'I know, I remember,' Father Joseph said, with a hint of pleasantness in his voice.

'Yes, well I just wanted to let you know where things stand at the moment. I'm sure you understand that when a report is made to us, it's our public duty to investigate it. The ramifications if we didn't would be... Well, it doesn't bear thinking about. Now, as you pointed out yesterday, we didn't find any evidence of any crime having been committed. That means there's a real possibility that someone has been making malicious allegations against you and the church, which I'm sure you'd like us to get to the bottom of,' Wendy said, trying to be as diplomatic as she could. 'Now, whoever made the phone call obviously knows the farm. They knew there was an old grain store, for example. That sounds like more than just guesswork to me.'

'You're good,' Father Joseph said.

Wendy wasn't quite sure how to react, so she chose not to. 'Which leads me to thinking that the person who made the call must have been here at some point. A former member of the church, perhaps.'

Father Joseph remained silent for a couple of moments before speaking.

'It's possible, I suppose,' he said.

'In which case, we can narrow down a list of suspects quite easily. Do you have a record of people who've lived at the farm in the past but have since left?'

Father Joseph smiled. 'Detective Sergeant Knight, a great many people have come through the doors of our church over the years. Yes, some have left. Those people lost their faith and need nothing more than the loving arms of God to save them. I do not wish to harm them by giving their names to the police.'

Wendy shuffled uncomfortably in her seat.

'But surely if these people are harming your church, you'd want to at least have the perpetrator identified, wouldn't you?'

'"For if you forgive other people when they sin against you, your heavenly Father will also forgive you",' Father Joseph said. 'Matthew, chapter six, verse fourteen.'

Wendy looked at him for a moment before speaking. Admittedly, it had been a while since her days at Sunday School, but it was her job to remember what people said — whether they were biblical or not. And she knew damn well what the next line was: *But if you do not forgive others their sins, your Father will not forgive your sins.*

'Do you see what this person — or people — did as a sin?' she asked him.

'Sin is a subjective concept, Detective Sergeant. It is not for me to decide what is a sin. The sins that matter are those that are sins in the eyes of the Lord.'

'Wrath is a sin, is it not? It seems like quite a wrathful act to make false accusations against a person, let alone a church.'

'Forgiveness trumps all,' Father Joseph replied with a smile. 'It is not for me to judge.'

Wendy could feel herself getting more irate — wrathful — as the conversation went on.

'No, but it is for me to judge whether a crime has been committed in the eyes of the laws of the country. And if I determine that it has, it's my responsibility to investigate it, identify the perpetrator and recommend them for prosecution.'

'And I would love to help you, but I'm afraid there's nothing I can do at this stage. We don't keep records of people coming and going. They are free to do as they wish.'

Wendy leaned forward. 'You must be able to name at least one person who's left the farm recently. Come on.'

'Detective Sergeant, all the people on this farm are my parishioners. I see them as my children. They are all one. Besides, what's in a name? It is God who will judge.'

'With the best will in the world, Father Joseph, God is unlikely to do much about this Himself.'

'Oh, I think you'd be surprised what God can do,' came the reply as Father Joseph steepled his hands. 'I think you'll find he can be very convincing indeed.'

13

Amy Kemp froze as she watched the policewoman walk back towards the entrance of the farm, accompanied by one of Father Joseph's henchmen. At least, that was the name she used to refer to them. Not out loud, of course. In a place like this, you never knew who you could trust. But it was obvious the woman was from the police. They'd been here before. It might have been yesterday, or the day before. They all tended to blur into one after a while.

This could be her chance. She'd long dreamed of the time she could get out of here, get away from the repression and subjugation, get away from all the despicable acts she'd been subjected to.

The first time, she was too young to understand what was happening. Her parents were overjoyed that she had been invited to a private audience with Father Joseph. It would be part of her initiation and her ticket into the infinite Kingdom of God. For a long time, she believed she must have done something wrong. Perhaps she hadn't put enough faith in God. Maybe that was why she was now being punished. Speaking of her punishment was never an option. That would have meant admitting to the sins that had led to her punishment. She didn't know what the sins were, which led her to assume they must have been truly dreadful, perhaps committed in a previous life.

It hurt like hell the first time. She was only seven years old. The second time was painful, the third time slightly less so. Before long, she learnt to block it all out. She used to sing nursery rhymes to herself in her head. She'd make up conversations with imaginary friends. And before she knew it, it was all over. She'd feel the weight of Father Joseph shifting off of her, followed by the gradual sensation of a warm stickiness between her legs.

Over time she'd learnt to realise what was going on. She didn't know why or how, but she'd grown a sense of self-awareness; a gradual realisation that something wasn't quite right, wasn't natural. Father Joseph must have sensed that realisation, because soon afterwards it all stopped. She hadn't been called in to see him again since.

She'd wanted to tell someone for so long, but knew it would be futile. Who, in here, would ever believe her? They all seemed completely devoted to Father Joseph and to the church. And those who expressed doubts were punished, if they were ever seen again. It was something she'd pushed to the back of her mind, knowing she would never be able to do anything about it. She had no options, no hope. But then she'd seen the policewoman.

They were almost at the gates now. She estimated that if she ran from here, she could reach the policewoman in about fifteen or twenty seconds. She could tell her everything, tell her about Father Joseph, about what went on in here. Her heart hammered in her chest just thinking about it. The possibilities were endless.

Before she could even realise what she was doing, she'd thrown open the door of the hut and was sprinting towards the gate and the policewoman. She ran past the grain store, past the chapel. She was just about to draw level with the small, white, brick-built building known as the medical centre when the large arm flung out and grabbed her round her waist, dragging her inside.

14

The first afternoon briefing of any investigation was often quite a busy one. Early plans of action had been put into place and information would be starting to come through. It was usually at these early briefings that the general direction of an investigation would start to become clear.

With this particular investigation, the mood was an odd one. It was standard for CID to get involved when there had been a death and there was a suspicion of foul play. In this case, though, there wasn't even a body to prove that anyone had even died. But with uniform resources being severely limited and a CID unit on hand in Milden-heath, it was often easier for uniformed officers to just dump it on Culverhouse and his team to cover their own arses.

'Right, settle down everyone,' Culverhouse said, before taking a mouthful of black coffee. 'Okay, let's start from the beginning. Stage one. A call comes in to us from an anonymous person telling us there's a dead body, potentially a murder victim, in the old grain store at Hilltop Farm. What have we got on that, Ryan?'

Ryan Mackenzie stood up and started to read from her notes.

'Well, I got onto the control centre and asked—'

'For fuck's sake. Sit down, will you? What do you think this is, the crown court?' Culverhouse barked.

'Sorry, sir. Just trying to be formal.'

Steve Wing let out a guffaw. 'Formal? Here? Don't make us laugh.'

Ryan chose to ignore him. 'I got onto the control centre and asked them for a transcription of the call. I've got the original audio, too. Transcription reads as follows. "Operator: Emergency, which service? Caller: Hi. Operator: Do you need fire, police or ambulance? Caller: Police. Operator: Connecting you. Operator: Hello, police emergency. Caller: Hi. Uh, there's a dead body. Someone's been murdered. At the farm. Operator: What address? Caller: Hilltop Farm. Operator: Hilltop Farm? And where's that? Caller: It's just outside Mildenheath. Operator: Do you have an address? Caller: No. No. No I don't. It's along from the Seafarer pub. Operator: There's a dead body on the farm? Caller: Yes. Operator: Whereabouts on the farm? Caller: The old grain store. Operator: There's a dead body in the old grain store? Caller: Yes. A woman. Operator: Where are you phoning from now? Caller: Uh, from a phone box. Please just send someone. Operator: We've got officers on the way. What's your name? Caller: No. I can't say. Please. It's a murder. Operator: It's a murder? Are you a witness? Caller: No. I can't tell you. Please. Operator: Sir, can you stay where you are? I'll send some officers to your location as well. They will be able to help you. Caller: No. No." Then he hangs up.'

'Very... thorough,' Culverhouse said. 'And what can we get from that? The caller doesn't have an address for the farm. If we're assuming the call came from someone who knows the farm well, or has been on it, wouldn't he know the address?'

'Dunno, sir,' Ryan replied. 'Not all farms have addresses as such. Just maybe a road name and near whatever town they're near.'

'Right. Well I don't think we can rule out that this was a hoax call. Not by any stretch of the imagination. I'd like nothing more than to walk into the chief constable's office with proof of that, believe me. Bloody waste of time. Frank, anything on the finances yet?'

'Not a thing, guv,' Frank Vine replied. 'Taking ages to get anything back from the banks. Usual story.'

'Keep me updated when you hear something,' Culverhouse replied. 'Knight. What did you get from Father Joseph Kümmel?'

Wendy took a deep breath. 'I wish I could answer that, sir. The short answer is not a lot. I found him pretty difficult to deal with, actually. He always seemed to know the right thing to say without actually saying anything. I can see exactly why he's running a cult.'

'Alternative church, Detective Sergeant Knight,' Culverhouse said.

Wendy looked at him, even though he wasn't looking at her. The brazen hypocrisy of the man was astounding.

'Right. Well whatever you want to call it, it seems pretty clear to me why he's so successful with it. Father Joseph was pretty standoffish when we went to see him on the original call yesterday. He was totally different today. Still evasive, but much calmer. Like he was trying too hard to be nice.'

'I'm not surprised,' Culverhouse replied. 'Yesterday he had a whole gang of us turn up unannounced, threatening to kick the gate in. Whereas today he gets visited by a young woman who just wants to ask him for a list of names. Doesn't take a mastermind to work out that he's going to respond a bit better to that, does it?'

Wendy stood open-mouthed in disbelief. The DCI would usually be the first person to spot something suspicious where there was nothing. He was probably the least tolerant person she knew, yet here he was defending Father Joseph Kümmel and whatever was going on at Hilltop Farm.

'Debbie,' he said, before Wendy could respond. 'What did you find out about the farm?'

'Went onto Google Earth like you said,' Debbie replied, holding up a sheet of paper with an aerial image printed on it. 'Can't see much, to be honest. There are a few buildings scattered about, but other than that it's difficult to make much out. It's not a great image. A lot of these satellite images were done years ago and haven't been updated since. To be honest, from above it just looks like a cross between a working farm and a holiday camp.'

'What about ownership?'

'Just heard back from the land registry a few minutes ago. It's been registered to the Community of Freedom and Enlightenment since May 1971.'

'Right. Who'd they buy it off and how much for?'

'No idea, sir. Land registry only started keeping title registers in 2000. We're going to have to dig a lot harder for any information like that.'

'In which case,' Culverhouse said, perching on the end of his desk, 'That's going to take up a lot of time and resources. We need to question if it's worth it. We're going to have to find out whether the claims made on the phone call are real or not. And quickly. Ryan, did you get anything from CCTV?'

'I've had uniform on the case, sir. Nothing residential that we've been able to find yet. The row of shops on Allerdale Road don't have anything, either. Most just cover the front of the shops. Two cover the slip road and parking area for the shops, but not Allerdale Road itself, and not the phone box. I'm currently mapping out where we do have CCTV coverage from shops, banks and residential addresses — as well as council-owned CCTV — and trying to block off areas where we should look. With any luck we'll be able to see a person or a car in the area at the right time. I'll get highways onto checking ANPR, too. There aren't any number plate recognition cameras in town itself, but there should be some on the main roads leading in and out. Might be useful if the caller came from out of town.'

'Excellent. Keep me posted. And someone get onto the voice experts, too. Get that recording of the phone call analysed. They'll be able to pick out accents, nervousness, all that. They'll probably even be able to tell us if the bloke was telling the truth or not. Save us a whole lot of hassle.'

Although it wasn't something she'd admit to very often, Wendy completely agreed with the DCI. She hoped beyond hope that the call would turn out to be a hoax. Because, if it wasn't, this whole investigation could turn out to be very messy indeed.

15

Father Joseph Kümmel clenched his jaw, his eyes burning into the wooden desk as he stared at it. If he wasn't careful, everything would come crumbling down around him. All the signs were there. First there was the incident with Isabella Martin. Then the police sniffing around. And now Amy Kemp's attempt at an opportunistic escape. Of course, there had been attempts and incidents in the past, but they were now growing in frequency. It was time for drastic action.

He signalled for Nelson to escort Amy Kemp's parents into the room and watched as the door opened, looks of awe and amazement on the Kemps' faces.

'Father Joseph, it is an honour to be invited to meet with you,' Mrs Kemp said, Father Joseph's raised hand silencing her just as quickly as she'd begun.

'My child, I have to tell you that I have not brought you here for happy reasons.' Father Joseph watched as Mr and

Mrs Kemp's faces changed, becoming bewildered and concerned. It gave him a kick. It made him feel powerful. 'I am sorry to say that Amy was taken ill earlier today. They took her to the medical centre, but there was nothing that they could do. She is with God now.' He scrutinised their faces, seeing them struggle between conflicting emotions and their deference to both him and to God.

'What... I don't know what you mean,' Mr Kemp said. 'Ill? How do you mean ill?'

'It is not for us to question God,' Father Joseph replied. 'But in my experience all the signs point to the involvement of the Devil himself. He will, when he sees fit, attempt to turn people. He will infiltrate their minds and their souls and poison them, making them ill and weak. And if we are unable to expunge him from within them, and we lose the battle, at least we know we will not lose the war.'

It was clear to Father Joseph that they didn't understand what he was saying, but that they were — as expected — hanging on his every word. They were good people. They were good disciples. Unfortunately for them, they had spawned a less than dedicated daughter. He could see the emotion starting to well up in Mrs Kemp.

'I understand this is a difficult time for you both,' Father Joseph said, 'but I feel it is important for you to know that your daughter did a good thing. She has highlighted the fact that the Devil is here, trying to do his evil work. Without her, we would not be aware of this. But I have to tell you, we are blessed with the spiritual and medical means to expunge the Devil from our community. Amy helped us to ensure that this was spotted at an early stage. She gave the ultimate sacrifice that the whole community might be saved. And you should be proud of that.'

Father Joseph held out his hands to Mr and Mrs Kemp, inviting them to hold a hand each. And he looked into their eyes as they took in what he was saying, unaware that this was going to get no better for them or for the community. Because Father Joseph was sure there could now only be one way out of this.

16

One of the perks of being the Senior Investigating Officer in CID was that overtime requests tended to get accepted more often than not. The county's Police and Crime Commissioner, Martin Cummings, had made serious and violent crime his main priority since being elected to his position. As far as Jack Culverhouse was concerned, that was the one good thing the PCC had done. He knew the time would come when overtime would be denied, as it had in the past. But that didn't bother him — he did it for the distraction rather than the money.

Besides which, he had work to do. Not work in the conventional sense, but work of his own.

He loaded up the familiar interface of the Police National Computer and went into the nominals database. He moved his mouse cursor over the text box and clicked, watching the cursor blink every second or so. He knew exactly what he wanted to type, but he also knew the potential ramifications of doing so. He wasn't worried about being caught — that could always be explained away, and in any case it was unlikely. His main worry was deeper than that. He was worried about breaking a bond of trust, a bond that was already pretty weak and which he'd already broken more than once.

But the possible outcomes of not doing anything could be far worse. Jack Culverhouse knew what went on in this town, and he knew the sorts of people who lived here. If there wasn't major crime, there was petty crime. It was one of those sorts of towns, and it didn't seem to be getting any better.

Jack knew that most people had a secret they wanted to hide. And in Mildenheath, that secret more often than not concerned the law. He wasn't only worried for Emily — he was worried for himself. A thirteen-year-old girl getting involved with a dodgy local family wouldn't look great for him. And it could potentially be more than dangerous for his daughter. The possibilities didn't bear thinking about.

So he didn't think about them. Instead, he looked down at his keyboard and tapped out Ethan Turner's name, before hitting the Enter key.

He didn't know what he'd been expecting to find. No match? A long list of convictions and charges? The first thing he noticed was Ethan's date of birth. He had turned eighteen four weeks previously. There was nothing major at first glance. There was a caution for shoplifting at the age of twelve, which on the face of it might not have looked like much but Jack knew was quite significant. Twelve-year-olds weren't just arrested, cautioned and added to the Police National Computer on a whim. That meant there was no way this had been his first run-in with the police. But since then, it seemed, he'd managed to keep his name away from the prying eyes of the police. Did that mean he'd gone on the straight and narrow? Culverhouse knew from experience that the answer was more than likely no. In this part of the world, very few people ever gave up a life of criminality. More often than not, it was a case of them getting wiser and ensuring that they didn't get caught any more.

He noted Ethan's home address — the Loriton estate in Heverstone. It was a familiar name — one that anyone on the local police force would know. In Jack's eyes, there was no way in hell Ethan Turner had decided to devote his life to cross-stitch and listening to *The Archers*. No, by now it would be soft drugs and pick-pocketing at the very least. Perhaps a bit of car theft or house burglary. Maybe some involvement in fraud somewhere along the line. Jack knew the patterns.

He made a mental note of Ethan's address and filed it away in his memory bank. He had a feeling he might be needing it.

17

Wendy knew a case was right for her when she got home from work and took a good couple of hours to wind down. Any other person might think their job was too pedestrian if they got home after a full day and wanted to spend an hour or two doing the housework and ironing. But Wendy was different. She knew herself well enough to know that this was a good sign. It meant the case was motivating her and keeping her energised — something all police officers lived for.

She knew damn well she was onto something with Father Joseph Kümmel, and she knew he knew it too. The only problem was that she had to convince Culverhouse. She had to find something that would save him from marking it down as a hoax call. She'd had all sorts of ideas flying into her head, most of them completely dreadful. She'd even thought for a moment about suggesting they send someone in undercover to pose as someone wanting to join the church. But she quickly realised just how bad an idea that was. Even if they got the clearance to pull an operation like that, it'd take an enormous amount of planning and would have a pretty low chance of success.

As far as Wendy could see it, they were stuck between a rock and a hard place. There was no hard evidence whatsoever of anything untoward going on at Hilltop Farm, but there was no way they could gather any evidence either. They had the power to go in and search the farm, but the place was huge and most of it was farmland. If it were a house, she reckoned they could piece together a search team and do the whole building inside a day. Hilltop Farm would take far, far longer. And that wasn't even taking into account the possibility that bodies could easily have been buried in the fields and crop patches. Loose, freshly dug earth wouldn't exactly be a rarity on a working farm. And there was no way they'd get the budget clearance to bring in the advanced gadgetry that could detect dead bodies underground. Not just based on one anonymous phone call.

Usually, that lack of evidence would be enough to satisfy Wendy that their response had been measured and appropriate. But something about Hilltop Farm concerned her.

Her eyes glazed over as the colours and shapes on the television mingled and merged. She wasn't even sure what she was watching — it was just background noise and something to have on while she zoned out. Her hand reflexively and rhythmically stroked her cat, Cookie, who purred in response.

The ringing of her phone jolted her back into reality. She looked down at the display and saw a withheld number. That meant it could well be work. She swiped her finger across the bottom of the screen to answer it.

The voice on the other end of the phone was polite, professional and matter-of-fact. It was a call she didn't think she'd ever expected to receive. The news itself wasn't a huge surprise, but it was something she'd shoved to the back of her mind, tried not to focus on. Now, though, she had no choice. She thanked the woman and ended the call.

She sat for a moment, gazing at the wall. She knew exactly what her response should be. It should be to ignore it, forget it and move on. But she had no choice. Her instinct overruled her. She had to be there.

She picked up her phone again and dialled Jack Culverhouse's number.

'Yeah?' he said, eventually, once he'd answered the call.

'Hi. It's me,' Wendy said, unsure what to say, the previous call still replaying in her mind.

'I know it's bloody you. The number came up on my screen,' Culverhouse replied. 'What do you want?'

Wendy swallowed and tried to think of the words. 'It's Michael,' she said. 'I had a call from the prison. He's been attacked.'

'Attacked?' Culverhouse replied. 'What do you mean?'

'I mean he's been bloody attacked!' Wendy shrieked, surprising herself at her reaction.

'Right,' came the response from the DCI, followed by a long silence.

'I need to go and see him,' Wendy said.

'See him? When?'

'Now.'

Wendy could hear Culverhouse sighing at the other end of the phone. 'Knight, he's in fucking Frankland. That's in Durham. It's a four hour drive from here.'

She could feel her patience running thin. 'I know where it is, guv. And yes, I'm going to need tomorrow off. Call it compassionate leave, call it what you like. He's my brother and I need to see him.'

There was a moment of silence before Culverhouse spoke. 'No.'

'No? What do you mean "no"?' Wendy asked, her voice rising.

'I mean no. You're needed at work. Unless it's life threatening, you're not entitled to compassionate leave. And anyway, let's face it. He's a scumbag murderer. He killed five women. And your bloody boyfriend. What the hell do you want to rush up there to see him for? So he's been given a slapping by another inmate. Boo fucking hoo.'

Wendy tried to keep a lid on her anger, but she could feel herself failing. 'You know what?' she said, finally. 'I don't give a shit what you say. I'm going up to see him and that's that. Put me down as absent without leave if you like. I couldn't care less.'

She ended the call, switched off her phone and grabbed her car keys from the hall table. She stopped only to look up at the clock. Four hours would get her to HMP Frankland well after midnight, but right now she really didn't care.

18

Ben Gallagher laid flat on his bed and stared up at the ceiling. There wasn't much light coming in through the curtains — just the glow of the moon — but it was enough to highlight the crawling damp that was creeping its way across the plasterwork. This whole place was going to shit. The sooner the better.

He'd long suspected what was happening to detractors, but he'd never seen it with his own eyes. Not until he saw someone snatch Amy Kemp.

He knew there was no way he was going to get to sleep. Not after what had happened over the past couple of days. From now on, he'd be sleeping with one eye open.

They had laid the plan long in advance, and it had been really quite simple. Simple, yet brazen. Ever since his brother Harry had escaped, he'd wondered where he'd got to, wondered what life was like for him on the outside — if he ever got to the outside. Six months or so later, one morning, things had started to become far clearer.

That morning, he'd got up as usual and gone up onto the herb garden to give the plants their morning water. The rooftop garden was the ideal place for growing herbs — it was high up and drenched in sunshine. Situated on top of the outbuilding which stored his gardening tools, it was where he grew herbs for the whole community. The rooftop garden was only accessible by way of a rickety wooden ladder at the side of the building, which Ben locked inside the outbuilding each evening. He didn't need to, but he did. As the person responsible for the herb garden — as well as other areas — he was the only person who went up there. The whole farm was single-storey — Father Kümmel was rumoured to be deathly afraid of heights — and Ben considered the rooftop garden to be his own private solitude.

He'd climbed the ladder, crawled onto the flat white roof and started to inspect the plants when he noticed something that hadn't been there the day before. On closer inspection, he could see it was a matchbox.

It took him a moment to process it. No-one came up here except him. He stored the ladder away each night, and only he had the key to the outbuilding. It was possible, he supposed, that someone could have thrown it up here from ground level if they were a good enough thrower. But that still didn't explain where they'd come from.

He picked up the matchbox and opened it. There was a folded sheet of paper inside, which Ben opened and read.

The message was in small print, scrawled in black pen on thin A4 notepaper.

Can't fit much on 1 sheet of paper. Restricted by weight. Have means of getting info in and out of farm. Write messages in chalk on roof garden. Will send camera drone over every Thursday during mass. Start this week. H

As he laid on his bed, he could still remember the feeling he had when he first read that. He knew immediately who it was from. Harry was out, and he was safe. The idea of sending information in and out of the farm petrified him, though. He knew he could trust his brother, but the thought of going against Father Kümmel and the church still frightened him half to death.

He'd read the note ten times over. He still wasn't sure what a camera drone was, but he'd got the gist of it. What messages did Harry want him to write? Thursday had been two days away, and he'd spent those two days thinking of what he'd write.

Finding the chalk hadn't been difficult. Hilltop Farm, like most of the Mildenheath area, was built on some of the chalkiest earth in Britain. It was everywhere. On the Thursday morning, he'd gone up onto the rooftop garden as he did every morning, and cleared a space in the centre. In that space, he'd written his message:

. . .

Got your note. Thanks.

He couldn't think of anything else to say. He had no information, no messages. At least, not at that stage.

Harry would sometimes drop notes of his own, always in matchboxes, and always scribbled on one sheet of thin paper. They'd always be concise, just as Ben's scrawled chalk messages had to be. Over time, they'd developed their own form of shorthand without even realising it. Over time, Ben had grown comfortable enough to express his dissatisfaction with life on the farm, especially when Harry had told him about life on the outside.

There was no way Ben would be able to escape. They both knew that. Harry had told Father Kümmel that he wanted to be a missionary, wanted to bring people to the church in the same way his father had been brought there more than two decades earlier. That had given Harry his chance to get on the outside and to escape. Ben would have no chance of being able to pull the same stunt. But, together, they would keep their finger on the pulse of Hilltop Farm and try and find some way of blowing the whole place open from the inside.

When Ben had seen, completely by chance, the body of Isabella Martin being carried towards the grain store, he knew they had something that could end the whole thing very quickly. He'd scrawled a message in chalk on the roof of the building and waited for Harry's camera drone to pass again. Then he'd sat back and watched as it all started to unfold.

His heart had sunk when he watched the police leave that day, with one lone officer returning the next day to tie up the loose ends. His hopes of bringing the whole church crashing to its knees had been dashed. How had they not managed to find Isabella's body? They were fucking police officers!

He closed his eyes for a few moments, feeling the back of his head rest on the rock-hard bed. When he opened them again, he looked back up at the mouldy ceiling and wished the whole thing would come crashing down.

But he knew he had another way out. He knew there was another way to smash this place open from the inside.

It was time for plan B.

19

Jack Culverhouse nursed a glass of whisky and stared hazy-eyed at the TV. The evening news was on — something about a banking scandal — but he wasn't paying much attention. He had more than enough on his mind.

When there was a big case at work he found himself being able to think quite clearly, methodically, working his way through it. It was only once the problems on his mind came from his personal life that he found himself unable to work out the best course of action.

One such problem was Wendy Knight. He'd had his concerns about her lately anyway, particularly considering her behaviour over the Hilltop Farm incident. What the hell was she thinking, trying to undermine him? And now, ringing him after work, telling him she was disappearing off to the North East in the middle of the night to visit her drug-addicted, serial-killing brother in prison. That was the final straw. He'd be having some serious words with her when she got back.

The whole incident had upset him far more than he'd realised. As far as he was concerned, he and Wendy hadn't had the best start to their working relationship. It'd be fair to say they rubbed each other up the wrong way more often than not. But he couldn't deny that she was a bloody good detective. Indeed, he'd considered recommending her for her Inspector's exams recently. Now, though, he was starting to reconsider.

To top all that, he couldn't shake Ethan Turner from his mind. What the hell was Emily doing running around with a kid like that? She should've been brought up to know better. After all, she was a policeman's daughter. The irony wasn't lost on him, though: It was the job that had caused him to lose Emily in the first place. If he hadn't been a police officer, he might not have lost her. But then she wouldn't have had the policeman father that she never had anyway. Whichever way he looked at it, he was always destined to lose.

He knew he needed to find out more about Ethan Turner, but he'd have to be very careful. It was a huge no-no to let your private concerns creep over into policing, and he knew he'd already overstepped the mark by looking Ethan up on the Police National Computer. But, at the same time, he knew a few officers in different divisions who'd be quite happy to spill the beans over a pint or a cup of coffee.

Half the problem, he knew, was that he still saw Emily

as this sweet young girl. She was a teenager now, and would be living a life of her own, making her own choices. But that didn't stop him from having this overwhelming protective urge. He wondered if he'd ever lose that feeling. Would it have been different if he'd been there to watch her grow up, be able to observe her maturing, develop some trust in her? He didn't know. There was no way he could ever know.

The sound of the front door opening jolted him back to reality. Emily walked through into the living room, looking like she'd just run a marathon.

'You alright?' Jack said, trying to hide the concern from his voice.

'Yeah, fine.'

'You don't look it,' he said, gesturing to her lank hair and wet clothes.

'It's raining. No biggie.'

'Where've you been? I would've happily given you a lift if you'd asked.'

'It's cool. Honestly. I like walking in the rain,' Emily said, heading for the kitchen.

He sensed that although Emily clearly had things on her mind, she also seemed a lot brighter. He considered that now might be a good time to broach the subject of Ethan Turner. He knew he'd have to be careful, though. One false move and he'd potentially lose the lot. He couldn't risk that. But at the same time he couldn't risk Emily getting involved with a juvenile criminal. Sure, she might never forgive him, might even disappear back to her grandparents again, but it would be worth it in the long run if it kept her safe.

He went into the kitchen after her, and watched as she spooned a heap of hot chocolate powder into a mug, the electric kettle bubbling away beside her.

'Look, Em, I think we need to talk,' Jack said, trying to sound as calm and positive as possible. He knew that getting all serious from the off wouldn't be the best way to approach the situation.

'Yeah. I think we do,' Emily replied, throwing him off balance for a moment.

'Right. Well the thing is, I know I've done stupid things and made plenty of mistakes. I know that. But I always want the best for you. Any father would.' Emily wasn't saying anything; just stirring her mug of hot chocolate. 'You know I just want to look out for you, right?'

'I know,' she whispered.

'I just want to look after you.'

'Dad, I know what you're saying. And I know what you're asking,' Emily said.

'You do?'

'Yeah. Look, I've been giving it some thought. I know I've only heard one side of things, and I know you're trying. I just... I really don't want to go back to Nan and Grandad's. I'd rather stay here with you. I'd like to give it a go.'

Jack glanced down at his daughter and saw the look in her eyes. All he'd wanted for so long was to hear her say she wanted to spend some time with him. And now here she was, telling him she wanted to stay with him and try to build a father-daughter relationship. He smiled, his lips pursed, desperate to handle his emotions. Of course, he was delighted, overwhelmed that she wanted to stay with him. But how could he broach the subject of Ethan Turner now?

He pulled Emily towards him and embraced her in a hug.

20

The Premier Inn was less than a mile and a half from HMP Frankland. Wendy'd had no choice but to book herself into the hotel as the prison were adamant that they wouldn't let her see Michael until the morning. She consoled herself that maybe this meant he hadn't been attacked too badly after all. But if that was the case, why had they called her? People were attacked in prison all the time; the places were full of violent criminals. This had to be something different.

It felt strange being in the hotel. Although it looked exactly like any other identikit Premier Inn anywhere across the country, this particular one had the distinction of being close to the prison where her brother had been housed for the past few years. She hadn't brought a change of clothes or an overnight bag. It hadn't even occurred to her that she might need them. She'd just grabbed her car keys and gone. As luck would have it, the hotel had been able to sell her a toothbrush and toothpaste — at an extortionate markup — so she had at least been able to brush her teeth.

She kicked off her shoes and laid back on the bed, propping a mound of pillows behind her, and switched on the TV on the other side of the room. She knew she needed to wind down somehow and get a couple of hours' sleep, but she also knew it wasn't going to be easy.

She didn't know how she felt. Not deep down. There was a mixture of worry, anger and sheer trepidation. She didn't even know if she actually wanted to see Michael again, but she knew she had to. If she was honest with herself, she thought it might be easier now that she was the one in control. If she could retain that control, that was.

21

Jack Culverhouse wasn't in the best of moods that morning as he slapped a pile of papers down on his desk and took a slurp from his coffee mug. He was never in a great mood in the mornings, but the prospect of having to sort out disciplinary proceedings against Wendy Knight was going to put an even bigger downer on things.

He didn't want to have to do it, but he didn't have much choice. Going AWOL from police duty wasn't looked upon too lightly by the powers that be, no matter who you were. But, of course, Jack could see her point of view. Even if he'd never tell her that. He'd not exactly been an angel himself at times, when it came to deciding which call of duty to answer. Sometimes one's real duty lay elsewhere.

His day was only about to get worse, though, when his phone started to ring. He looked down at the display and recognised the number immediately. It was one he'd seen flash up on his phone quite a bit over the years — the number of the local newspaper, the Mildenheath Gazette.

'Sorry, I'm not entering the crossword competition this week,' he barked as he picked up the phone.

'DCI Culverhouse, Suzanne Corrigan,' the reporter said, ignoring his attempt at a joke.

Culverhouse and Suzanne Corrigan had had dealings together in the past, most notably when Suzanne had been the fifth intended victim of a local serial killer. The showdown at her house had resulted in the untimely death of DS Luke Baxter, whom Culverhouse had considered his protégé.

'Morning,' Culverhouse replied, not even wanting to go so far as to ask what she wanted. Truth be told, he didn't care. The press could verge on being vaguely useful on occasions, but more often than not he tended to see them as a hindrance.

'I'm just ringing about a report we had from a local resident, actually. I wondered if I might be able to discuss it with you.'

'You'll have to be quick. I've got a meeting in ten minutes,' Culverhouse lied.

'It won't take long. Just want to clear up a few facts. It's to do with Hilltop Farm. Do you know it?'

Culverhouse's heart sank. He knew it, alright. 'I have a vague recollection, yes,' he said, taking a deep breath and speaking as calmly as he could.

'Well I got a weird call late last night, just as I was about to leave. From someone who wanted to give us some information on a religious cult that's based on the farm. He said he was a former resident there and wanted to "lift the lid" — his words — on what goes on there.'

Culverhouse's interest was suddenly piqued. 'Did you get his name?' he asked, presuming this was the same caller who'd reported the non-existent body on the farm.

'No, he wouldn't tell me. He said he wanted to speak to me a bit first. I think he's worried about repercussions.'

Culverhouse made a non-committal noise. If the man was worried about repercussions, that meant there was something to be afraid of. Or, he could want to avoid identifying himself because it was all one huge lie or hoax. Either way, it wasn't looking great. 'Right. What did he say?'

'Well, that's just it. He didn't say much. Between you and me, I think he was sounding me out, seeing how seriously I'd take him before he got to the really juicy stuff. But there was one thing he mentioned,' Suzanne said, trailing off, trying to whet Culverhouse's appetite. He didn't take the bait. A couple of seconds later, she continued. 'He said he'd reported an incident to the police recently, in which he gave information about a death on the farm. A murder, he called it. He said his call wasn't taken seriously.'

Culverhouse sighed. 'Look, you know I can't discuss ongoing cases with you. Not unless I have specific clearance to do so.'

'So there *is* an ongoing case, then?' Suzanne asked.

'I didn't say that.'

'So you *can* discuss it with me?'

Culverhouse clenched his jaw. Journalists had a habit of being able to tease a front-page story out of nothing, but this was pushing it. 'Off the record,' he said, knowing damn well that nothing was off the record with journalists, 'we received an anonymous phone call from someone telling us there was a body on the farm. We attended, searched the scene and found no evidence of said body. The phone call couldn't be traced and we saw no sign that any crime had been committed. As such, no further investigation has taken place.'

'A very concise and media-friendly response, considering it's off the record,' Suzanne said. Culverhouse noted that she'd grown in confidence following the recent Ripper case, which had nearly ended her career and her life.

'You know me, Suzanne. I'm always friendly to the media.' He could swear he heard her stifle a laugh.

'So I can use that quote in the paper, can I?'

'No you fucking cannot,' he said, his voice harsh but low as he cradled the mouthpiece to avoid being overheard. 'And what's more, if you run a story about Hilltop fucking Farm, you'll have one very angry Detective Chief Inspector and one very litigious church leader on your back. Father Joseph Kümmel is not the sort of person who's likely to forgive something like that.'

'That's his name, is it? Kümmel? How do you spell it?' Suzanne asked.

Culverhouse clenched his jaw again. 'Fuck off,' he replied, before slamming the phone down. If he thought he was in a bad mood when he got to the office, it was nothing compared to how he felt after the phone call. He had to let off some serious steam.

He sat down in his chair and tried to calm himself. He knew rising stress levels were no good for him, but that was all words and theory. What was he meant to do? Just sit back and take it? Let it wash over him? No. That wasn't possible. First there was the Hilltop Farm fiasco, then Wendy Knight buggering off without leave, then the local papers getting on his back. And that was without worrying about all the shit he had to deal with in his personal life, with his ex-wife running off again and his hormonal young daughter coming to live with him out of the blue.

To him, Emily was the one good thing in his life right now. Even the job was starting to lose its appeal. But he knew he was in danger of losing her again. He could still see the old Emily inside her — the young daughter he once knew. That was a side of her he could see diminishing, though — particularly if she carried on hanging around with people like Ethan Turner. He'd already lost Emily once, and he wasn't going to risk losing her again. Before he could even think about what he was doing, he took his suit jacket off the back of his chair, put it on and grabbed his car keys.

22

The frontage to HM Prison Frankland was imposing to say the least, particularly in the half-light of the early hours. Wendy had been able to obtain special dispensation to visit her brother, partially because of the ferocity of the attack he'd been on the receiving end of, and partially because she was a serving police officer connected with the case that had convicted him.

The prison was notorious for housing some of the country's most dangerous criminals. It had been home to Charles Bronson, often referred to as the most violent prisoner in Britain. Harold Shipman, the most prolific serial killer in history in terms of proven victims, which tallied 218, had been incarcerated here too. Current inmates included Peter Chapman, the so-called 'Facebook killer'; Peter Sutcliffe, the Yorkshire Ripper; and Ian Huntley, the convicted sex offender and murderer of two young schoolgirls, Holly Wells and Jessica Chapman.

As a category A prison, Frankland was home to Britain's most dangerous and violent inmates. Wendy had known from the moment of Michael's arrest that he'd likely end up in a category A prison such as this. But realising that he was living in the same space as people such as the Yorkshire Ripper was something she found difficult to come to terms with. That was why, she supposed, she'd been blocking it from her memory for so long. It was a case of having to. A coping mechanism, of sorts. Because if you let it get to you, that was the sort of thing that could break you.

On entering the prison, Wendy went through the usual routine of being searched, identified and permitted entry. It was something she'd done many times before in various prisons as part of her job, but this was different. This time she wasn't here on work. She was here to see the brother she hadn't laid eyes on since that day in court.

Once the formalities had been dealt with, a female prison guard led Wendy through towards the Healthcare Centre.

'So what can you tell me?' Wendy asked her, keen to find out exactly what had happened, what she should expect.

'Not a whole lot, I'm afraid. I'm just your escort to the ward. I don't know any details. You'll have to ask the medical staff.'

Wendy clenched her teeth. She had no idea what to expect.

The Healthcare Centre contained, amongst other

things, a ward consisting of four beds. Wendy estimated there were a dozen or so private rooms. It was one of these rooms that Wendy was led to, a male prison guard keeping watch at the doorway. She presumed this must be because of the nature of Michael's injuries. If he'd been attacked by fellow inmates, it was right that he be kept isolated in a private room with some sort of protection.

She paused for a moment, looking back at the female prison officer who'd led her to this point.

'Uh, can I go and get a glass of water or something first, please?'

The prison officer looked at her for a couple of seconds, then gave a benevolent smile. 'Sure,' she said. 'Come with me.'

They walked a little further up the corridor and into a small kitchenette area. The prison officer took a glass from the over-sink cupboard and filled it from the cold tap.

'Listen, I haven't seen him. Michael. I don't know what's happened exactly, but all I can say is it might be best to prepare yourself for the worst. I spent a bit of time on the floor a couple of years back and saw one or two attacks. They're never pretty. We're not exactly talking petty criminals in here.'

Wendy gulped down the glass of water. 'Thanks. I'm just... I don't know what to expect. I haven't seen him since he got sent down.'

The prison officer nodded. 'He'll be different,' she said, trying to sound reassuring.

'Different?'

'Everyone's different in here. If they're big-time serial re-offenders like your Sutcliffes and your Bronsons, their bravado goes through the roof. Frankland's just another badge. For your one-offs and "we never would have suspected him" types, like your Huntleys and your Chapmans, they tend to get more isolated, more withdrawn. Prison'll change and accentuate anyone's personality pretty sharpish. It's what confinement does to a person.'

Wendy still wasn't sure what the woman meant, but by now she was too afraid to ask. Just hearing Michael mentioned in the same sentence as notorious monsters like that was enough to make her desperate to change the subject.

Back on the ward, Wendy tried to ignore the guard outside Michael's room and felt her heart skip as the prison officer opened the door. She walked in, keeping her eyes on the floor until she got towards the bed. She swallowed hard and realised she was holding her breath as her eyes drew upwards, up the bed and onto the figure that was in it.

Michael looked different, to say the least. He'd put some weight on in prison. It was weight he could afford to add compared to his former skinny frame, but Wendy could tell from the colour of his flesh that much of it was bruising and swelling. If she'd seen him in any other bed or hospital, she doubted she would have recognised him as her brother. He'd cut his hair much shorter than she'd ever seen before. There were marks and scars which were new to her, but clearly not from this most recent attack. She winced as she imagined how many scrapes he must've got into in here. He'd never been the violent type. Wendy knew that was a bizarre thing to say, bearing in mind his criminal history. But starting fights with inmates really didn't seem like Michael.

She realised she was starting to feel sorry for him, the way anyone would do if they saw their little brother lying beaten in a hospital bed. She had to steel herself and remember that, regardless of blood, this was the man who'd killed her boyfriend. The man who'd murdered innocent women. But that all fell by the wayside as Michael rolled his head towards her, opened his eyes and smiled at her.

'Hello Wend.'

23

Father Joseph Kümmel addressed the congregation with a calm, bass-laden voice that exuded a composed authority. He watched as the assembled parishioners took in his every word, each one of them looking at him as he spoke. He'd always loved hearing his voice reverberating around these walls, listening to the echoes of his deep timbre as it ricocheted off the cold stone, knowing it would also be reverberating through the skulls of the assembled parishioners.

It was all part of it. It was all psychology and body language. When it came to it, for all humanity's Nobel prizes and achievements, we were still just animals. And simple animals, at that. The truth was that we never actually *evolved* into the beings we are now. Not in the strict sense of the word. We just added more layers. We learned to make fire, we learned to develop language, we learned to engineer. But none of that replaced our basest animal instincts. Why were we attracted to different people?

Because we want to breed with them. Because we saw physical characteristics in them that we want our children to have. Why are we driven by revenge and greed? Because we are territorial mammals, chemically designed to want to look after our closest flock. Fight or flight, survival of the fittest. They're all our basest animal instincts, ones we had as cavemen, ones that never really evolved. We just papered over the cracks.

Human emotional contagion was one of those animal instincts which remained. It was how hysteria was spread, how wars were started. And it was a damn fine way to control people.

'There are eighty-six of us here in this church,' he said. 'Eighty-six. We are the only eighty-six people who have heard the true word of God. The only eighty-six people who can save this world from going down the path it is currently following. It is a world filled with greed, with jealousy, with hatred. Together, we have grown, both in size and in wisdom. Through our mutual love we have learned to spurn the outside world and develop our own world of tolerance, equality and knowledge of our Lord God. We are all honoured to have been shown that path of light, to be able to experience the love of God.

'But there are people who want to do us harm. People who benefit from the greed, jealousy and hatred of the outside world. People who thrive on those three things. People who are part of the forces of evil. A message of love, tolerance and equality is not something they want to see. It is anathema to everything they believe in. That is why they want to destroy us.'

Father Joseph looked around at the congregation. Heads were nodding, others looked concerned. The body language seemed right. He had them where he wanted them. He felt that familiar buzz of being in complete control. It was a buzz he'd had many thousands of times before, but of which he would never grow tired.

'In recent days we have seen the forces of evil far closer to home than we would have liked. The Devil has managed to worm his way in, warping the minds of some who were our brothers and sisters. Which is why,' he said, raising his voice for dramatic effect, 'we need to be more vigilant now than ever before. We cannot afford to rest on our laurels. Thus I ask you, watch over your loved ones. Watch over your families. Watch over the community. And should you see any sign of the Devil doing his evil work, come to us, for we can cleanse their souls.'

Father Joseph lowered his voice again, looking each of the congregation in the eye as he spoke. 'For evil will not triumph. We will take our knowledge and our salvation to the Kingdom of Heaven before the Devil can even get his foot in the door.'

24

The Loriton estate wasn't somewhere many officers would go to single-crewed. And it wasn't somewhere Jack Culverhouse would have normally fancied going at all, no matter how many people he was with. It was the sort of area where police weren't welcome. Many of the residents on the estate had had run-ins with the law in the past. Others felt the system in general had let them down, giving them a deep distrust of authority.

There were a few people out and about — a middle-aged woman walking a dog, two men in jeans and t-shirts, a group of children on bikes. Nothing to give him too much cause for concern, but even so he didn't want to be hanging around here for too long.

He slowed down as he reached the rough location he presumed Ethan Turner's house to be. He looked over and confirmed the house number, before driving a little further up the road and pulling over.

He sat in his car for a few moments, realising he hadn't planned any of this. What was he doing? What did he expect to achieve? It went without saying that his ultimate goal was for Emily to be safe and kept far away from potential criminality. His interest in that was twofold: he wanted to protect his daughter and his career. It wouldn't cause an automatic issue in his job if Emily had links to criminals. But it would be more fuel for the fire as far as people like Martin Cummings and Malcolm Pope were concerned.

But what could he do about it? If the force of the law couldn't stop someone carrying out criminal activities, what hope did he have on his own? What was he going to do? Knock on his door and ask him to be a good boy? He couldn't ask Emily to stop seeing Ethan. There's no way she'd understand. The smart option would be to give Ethan enough rope to hang himself with and be there for Emily when it all fell apart.

A large part of him, he had to admit, wanted to walk up to Ethan Turner's house, knock on his door, wait for him to answer and punch him in the face. It'd do nothing beneficial, but it'd make him feel a whole lot better. And it'd probably result in him losing both his daughter and his job — the two things he had come here to protect.

As he mulled it all over in his mind, his attention was drawn to movement in his wing mirror. He saw two people coming out of what he believed to be Ethan Turner's house. One was a lad of around seventeen or so. He guessed the other was around three or four years older, knowing how difficult it was to age teenagers. Take Emily, for example. He knew exactly how old she was, yet she looked and acted a good few years older. It was likely that either one of these lads could be Ethan Turner.

He watched as they crossed the road and got into a red Vauxhall Astra. A few seconds later, the car started to move and drove past Jack, reached the end of the road and turned left. As it did so, Jack started his car and sped to the end of the road, turning left and trying to get the red Astra back in his sights as soon as possible.

There was another car between them. That was good. It meant he was less likely to be seen, but could still keep the car in his sight. They came to a roundabout, and the Astra took the second exit. The car between them carried on round the roundabout. Jack followed the Astra, keeping a respectable distance and trying to observe the car without looking too obvious.

He knew this road linked the Loriton and Sholebroke estates. Neither of them were particularly desirable places to live. It wasn't an area he was familiar with. Knowing an area like the back of your hand had its advantages in policing. Right now, Jack was at a serious disadvantage in that regard.

A couple of minutes later, the Astra indicated and pulled over outside a public park. Jack continued driving and took the next right. He parked up outside a row of shops, got out of his car and locked it. He jogged back to the junction and headed towards the park, just in time to see the two lads enter the kids' play area. Two other men — both a bit older — were stood in there, leaning against a climbing frame. Jack watched as the two lads from the Loriton estate approached them. They seemed to all know each other, judging by the bizarre 'street' handshakes they were doing.

He was nowhere near close enough to hear what the lads were saying. He didn't want to risk getting any closer and spooking them. Even so, he'd been around long enough to know damn well what was going on. One of the older lads glanced around, seeming to be casing the area for witnesses. He dipped a hand into his pocket and handed something over to one of the Loriton boys. Jack couldn't see what it was, but he thought he saw one of the Loriton boys hand something else back the other way. To Jack, it looked like a classic drugs deal. He watched as they did the handshakes again, before the Loriton boys started to make their way back towards the car.

As they passed through the entrance gate to the park, Jack walked up to meet them.

'Ethan Turner?' he called out, not sure which one was him. That uncertainty was soon resolved, though, as one of the boys looked up at him immediately. Culverhouse couldn't hide his anger and resentment any longer. 'I want to have a word with you,' he said, walking closer towards him.

'Shit! Run!' the other lad yelled, before both turned to sprint in the direction of the car. Just as Jack started to go after them, the boy he'd identified as Ethan tripped. He skidded along the pavement on his side, groaning in pain. Jack was on him in moments. He looked up just in time to see the other lad have to make a decision over whether to help him or continue his escape. Fortunately for Jack, he chose the latter, and sped off in his car, back towards the Loriton estate. The two older lads in the park had also started to run away from him, up towards the top end of the park. Jack was grateful for the element of surprise. Even if they'd realised he was a police officer, there could be dozens of them behind him for all they knew.

'Nice friends you've got there, Ethan. Loyal,' Jack said as he pushed his knee further into Ethan Turner's back and dialled the number of the station. 'Maybe you might like to meet mine instead.'

25

Father Joseph's tone during the most recent sermon worried Ben. The sermon had been unexpected, although he had a fair idea of what he should expect after seeing Amy Kemp being snatched mid-run.

He'd watched it all. He'd almost been able to read what was going through her mind. He could almost see the cogs turning. He'd been tempted himself a few times, but he knew the risks were too high. The only way he was ever going to get out was by playing the long game. Good things come to those who wait.

Father Joseph and his cronies had one enormous advantage: by and large, they were trusted. That meant they could get away with doing all sorts of things, even in broad daylight, and people would either turn a blind eye or they'd not even see it. But Ben was different. Ben was watching.

He'd been watching, too, when Amy Kemp had tried to make a run for it. He'd seen her dash towards the policewoman. He watched as she ran past the door to the medical centre and straight into the arms of one of Father Joseph's henchmen. He hadn't seen who.

Calling it a medical centre was a joke. It was a damp white brick building, freezing cold even in the height of summer, and had been constructed purely to make the community feel safe. Ben never went anywhere near there, even when he was unwell. He'd far rather lie and hope whatever it was would sort itself out. He couldn't bear to go into that horrendous building and be subjected to whatever false science Dr Joseph and his cronies were espousing that week.

Ben was well aware that he didn't have a working concept of what real medicine was like, but he wasn't exactly sheltered either. No-one in the community was. Enough of the people living here had lived on the outside to be able to make the comparison. Many were able to talk — in private — about the differences between life on Hilltop Farm and on the outside. Only a few were born and raised on the farm with no workable concept of the outside world.

Discussions weren't often had about comparing Hilltop Farm to the outside world, though. Rumours were rife of other people — even friends and family members — reporting those sorts of transgressions to the powers that be. Father Joseph's whole ethos was that the parishioners were happy to be here. That they had free will. Ben knew that was bullshit.

No-one thought life here was perfect. Well, perhaps there were one or two of the more dedicated and devoted community members who wore the rose-tinted glasses. But, on the whole, the feeling was that life was still better here, with its leaky buildings and damp floors, than it was on the outside. There was no greed, no envy. The seven deadly sins didn't exist at Hilltop Farm. Everyone was equal. Sure, they didn't have cars, didn't have televisions, didn't have computers. But that was all *stuff*, and not only that but stuff they didn't truly want. It was a material distraction, intended to keep the masses happy and ignorant of the fact that their world was driven by corporate greed and corruption. It wasn't a utopia by anyone's standards, but its advantages were deep-rooted and its disadvantages material.

That was what kept the community so dedicated to itself, so reverent of Father Joseph Kümmel. Nowhere else could they live in a way which allowed them to remain 'off the grid', not beholden to banks or corporations, living as freely — in a spiritual sense — as they could be. Ben had to admit that there was a certain romance to that, but it wasn't for him. Or, rather, it would have been for him had the greed and corruption not managed to worm its way into Hilltop Farm in the same way as it did everywhere else.

When the realisation had started to dawn that Father Joseph and his henchmen were not spiritual saviours but were the same corrupt, self-driven bastards as were every-where else, the novelty had worn off. He'd felt gutted, betrayed. And discovering that they could be killers, too, had sealed the deal for him.

Father Joseph's sermon had made Ben realise that something big was about to happen. The words reverber-ated around his head.

We will take our knowledge and our salvation to the Kingdom of Heaven before the Devil can even get his foot in the door.

He had taken that to mean only one thing: that Father Joseph considered an honourable death to be preferable to submitting to the outside world. And if the outside world was going to be breaking its way into Hilltop Farm regard-less, if they could not stop the tide, there was only one way out in Father Joseph's mind.

He'd wondered whether that was the endgame for a while now. Could Father Joseph really command so much respect that he'd be able to enable an enormous, wide-scale mass suicide? Ben was almost certain Father Joseph had convinced some former parishioners to take their own lives. He thought of Isabella Martin, knowing damn well what had happened there. He'd had his suspicions for a while, but that had confirmed them in his mind. And what now of Amy Kemp? Had she been forced to do the same? What if she'd refused?

He put down the metal watering can and eyed the space in the centre of the rooftop herb garden. The dark flat roof was stained grey with the numerous washed-off applications of chalk. He picked up another piece of chalk that he'd secreted in a plant pot, knelt down and started to write another message.

He knew he had to make it good. He knew this message could be his last.

26

He was the only person who ever called her Wend. As he said it, it took her right back to those times when they were younger, playing at their family home. Her parents used to hate anyone shortening her name, and she wasn't particularly keen on it herself. When Michael did it, though, it was almost sweet.

Was.

Now, it evoked memories of her first major case with Mildenheath CID. She'd nursed Michael through his drug addiction only to discover that he had been the murderer all along. She looked at him lying in his hospital bed, in one of the most notorious prisons in Britain, almost unable to comprehend what he'd become. That sweet, innocent young child. Troubled, yes. Weak, definitely. But she'd never expected him to become a monster.

'You don't want to talk to me. I get it,' Michael said, not breaking eye contact. 'But it's good to see you.'

Wendy didn't have a clue what to say. She'd never made any specific vow to herself never to see Michael again — it just wasn't something that had ever been on the cards. Why would it be, after all he'd done? She'd come a long way since she'd last seen him. She'd grown as a person and a police officer. Seeing him again now felt like it was dragging her back to the person she'd been back then.

'I wish I could say the same,' she replied, trying to keep her voice low and the emotion minimal.

Michael looked away for a moment. 'You obviously came for a reason, Wend. You can't tell me you were just passing.'

She had come for a reason. She knew that much. But she had no idea what that reason might be. 'I suppose I want answers,' she said, eventually.

'You didn't speak in court,' Michael replied.

'No. I didn't.'

'And what do you want answers to? How do you think I'm going to help exactly?'

Wendy shook her head. 'I don't know. I don't know anything right now, Michael. All I know is that I can't make sense of anything. I can't make sense of what happened to you, why you did it. How sudden it all was. Unexpected. I don't know. Just... Just why?' She could feel the emotion building up inside her, and tried to push it back down. She'd done a good job of repressing it for the past five or so years and she was going to carry on.

'Does it matter?' Michael asked, as if he'd just been asked what he had in his pockets.

'What do you mean?'

'Well, what difference will it make? It happened.'

'Because normal people need answers. That's what difference it'll make.'

'What, you mean *closure*?' Michael said, almost sneering the last word.

'Yeah, if you like. I prefer to call them answers, but whatever.'

'Read the court papers.'

Wendy was trying incredibly hard to keep a lid on her emotions. She was angry — furious — at Michael's lack of remorse. She was confused at the enormous change in his personality and devastated at the little brother she'd lost. They'd always been a close family. But the deaths of her parents and the complete personality transplant in Michael had ruined all that history and her happy memories. And she held Michael responsible for that.

'So what happened to you?' she asked, trying to change the subject and make her journey up here hold at least some value. 'Who did this?'

Michael gave something approximating a shrug. 'Other inmates. Obviously.'

'But why? Why you?'

'Why not? That's the type of people they are. It's what they do. They know why I'm here. They know who I am. It's what happens. This is my life now.'

Wendy felt her heart sink a little further. 'And are you happy with it?'

'What's happy?' Michael asked, after a couple of seconds of silence.

'It's what I've been recently,' she replied through gritted teeth. 'I've been getting my life back in order. Just about. I've got a new place. Work's going well. Not that you'd care.'

Michael said nothing.

'I found out I was pregnant,' Wendy said, feeling her eyes misting. 'Not long after you were caught. It was Robert's.' She took a deep breath, trying to hold back the tears. 'I went back to work sooner than I should have done. Far sooner. I needed to get my mind focused again. I was hiding from what had happened. I was chasing a suspect. There was an altercation, sort of. I tripped. I fell in the road and was hit by a car. I lost the baby,' she said, almost whispering. 'First I lost her father, then I lost her.'

'And you hold me responsible,' Michael said, flatly.

'I lost you too, Michael. I lost it all. And so did you. All because of... Well, only you know the answer to that.'

Michael was silent for a few moments. Wendy half-hoped he was thinking about it, trying to formulate an answer for her. Then again, with the time he'd spent inside he'd had plenty of time to think about it. If he didn't have an answer to that question by now, he probably never would.

As she had expected, he ignored the point altogether.

'Why did you bother coming up here, Wend?'

Wendy took a deep breath. 'Do you want me to be honest? I don't know. I really don't know. Maybe it was instinct. Instinct that when someone calls you to say your brother's been attacked, you want to go to him. Maybe it's an instinct I need to try and iron out of myself. Because it's clearly not one worth having any more.'

'You think I'm not grateful,' Michael said, quietly. It was difficult for Wendy to pick any sort of emotion out of what Michael was saying. It was all so flat, and gave her nothing to work with. Whether it was the result of painkillers, some other form of medication or just the effect of his incarceration, he was just lifeless.

'Well, forgive me if I'm wrong but you don't sound particularly grateful to me,' she replied. 'You don't sound like anything. You certainly don't sound like the brother I once knew. You're a completely different person.'

She could see she was getting nothing from him. She was on the verge of standing up and leaving, considering it a wasted journey, when she caught the light glinting off a solitary tear running down his cheek. His head was tilted to the side on his pillow, eyes glassy, staring at the wall. It was the first time in a long time she'd seen any sort of emotion from him. He looked vulnerable.

'Michael? Michael, what is it?' she asked, expecting to be ignored or for Michael to change the subject.

He rolled his head back towards her, before looking her in the eye.

'I need help.'

27

Amy Kemp listened to the pattern of her heartbeat, noticing that it roughly matched the throbbing of her head. If she didn't know better, she'd think her head was the only thing she had left, as it was all she could feel. Laid on her side, her legs tied together and her arms bound behind her back, everything was numb from the cold. The chill concrete floor was hard, and she wondered if the circulation to her limbs had been completely cut off.

She sent signals to her fingers and toes, trying to get them moving. She had no idea if it was working or not. Everything was numb. She knew her body would be starting to shut down soon, trying to conserve energy. She wondered how long a person could go without food or water before the inevitable happened.

She didn't remember much. One minute she was running hell for leather towards the policewoman. The next thing she knew, she was waking up here on the cold concrete floor. She knew she should be panicking. She knew she should be fearing for her life. But, deep down, she knew she had nothing to fear. After all, they could have killed her already by now. Why hadn't they? Why was she not already dead? To her, it was clear that they wanted her alive for some reason, whatever that reason might be. That gave her hope, but it also worried her. If they didn't want her dead, what did they want her for?

She thought back to those times when she was younger, with Father Joseph forcing himself on her. Surely that wasn't what they had planned, was it? No. It was impossible. He'd stopped all that with her long ago. She'd always presumed she was too old now.

Amy had always wondered whether other young girls had experienced the same things with Father Joseph. Whether they'd had to go through the same rituals, the same pain. Or had she been special, somehow? Sometimes she convinced herself that was the case. It was easier to assume that things were being done because *she* was the variable. The alternative — that Father Joseph was somehow a sexual deviant who'd been misleading the entire community and pretending to be something he wasn't — was far too huge a concept for a young girl to comprehend. But as she'd got older, she'd started to wonder.

She wriggled, trying to get the blood to flow into her limbs. She needed to make sure she still had them. She took in a deep breath, feeling the icy cold air fill her lungs. She coughed, pain searing through her chest as she did so.

The cold wouldn't help either. That would only be adding to the numbness. Within a few seconds of wriggling she felt the blood starting to push through her veins, the pain increasing with every pulse, the warm blood thawing the ice that had formed inside her limbs. It felt like electricity was flowing through her. It hurt like hell, and she far preferred it when she was numb, but she knew it was good for her. She knew she had to do it.

She tried to keep as quiet as possible, although all she really wanted to do was scream. It'd be a deep, guttural scream; a universal roar that would convey deep animalistic anguish to any creature within a mile or two. But she knew she had to keep quiet. She had to let them believe they'd won.

Deep down, she wondered if they already had.

28

Although Jack Culverhouse was far more suited to CID work these days, there was still nothing quite like a good old-fashioned nick. A bit of a chase, a rugby tackle and a face pressed against the concrete. It took him right back to his days on the beat.

He knew he couldn't get involved in interviewing or charging Ethan. It would look far too bizarre for a CID officer to be processing a small-time drugs arrest, and he didn't particularly want to have his name on Ethan's charge sheet. He'd let one of the uniformed officers have the arrest as far as the paperwork went, which would keep his own name off the system.

He'd told the custody sergeant the truth, but had decided to leave out large parts of the story. He mentioned being on the Sholebroke estate and seeing something suspicious in the park. He told the custody sergeant his instincts took over and he'd gone in for the kill. Fortunately for him, neither the custody sergeant nor the uniformed constables felt comfortable asking him why he'd been on the Sholebroke estate in the first place.

The process for arresting and charging most people was the same. An officer would arrest them, bring them to the local police station and have them booked in by the custody sergeant. At that point, the clock would start ticking. The police would then have twenty-four hours to either charge or release the suspect. In that time they'd conduct interviews, gather evidence and consult the Crown Prosecution Service. The ultimate decision to charge or release came from the CPS. Their remit was to ensure that flimsy cases didn't reach the expense of having to go to trial. For that reason, they had to discover, gather and process the evidence inside twenty-four hours, and it had to be rock solid.

Fortunately for Jack, the evidence against Ethan Turner was pretty strong. They'd found him with a small amount of cannabis on him and he'd admitted to buying the drug for personal use. As it was the first drugs offence that Jack knew of, he was likely to be cautioned and released without a formal charge. It'd go on his criminal record, but he wouldn't have a sentence or even a day in court. Had they caught him a few weeks earlier, while he was still a minor, they wouldn't have been able to arrest him for the offence at all.

The main thing was that he'd be back on the system again. He'd be a known name, would find it harder to get a job and would, hopefully, decide that breaking the law just wasn't worth it. He also hoped that Emily would somehow find out on the grapevine what he'd been up to and stop hanging around with him. He knew teenage minds didn't always work that way, but right now it was his only hope. And, on the plus side, he'd taken the cannabis out of Ethan Turner's possession, keeping it away from Emily. It wasn't much, but it was a start.

His private life put to one side for a moment, he tried to wrap his head around the stack of papers on his desk. He needed to get his brain back into work mode, but it wasn't easy. Other things kept getting in the way.

He tried to focus his mind on the investigation into Hilltop Farm. As far as he was concerned, it was all a complete waste of time. The investigation had stalled before it had even started, but he had no real option. If the powers that be wanted it investigated, he didn't have a choice. As long as he could make it look like something was being done, then come back to them in a few days and tell them they'd found no evidence of any wrongdoing, his arse would be covered. And then he could get back to investigating real crime.

His desk phone started to ring. Looking down, he saw the call was coming in from the main call handling team.

'Culverhouse.'

'Hi. I just received a call from a Dr Magnus Pedersen,' the woman on the other end of the phone said. 'He said he was calling for you because your wife has been admitted to hospital. You were listed as her next of kin.'

Jack's heart skipped a beat. 'Hospital? What for?' He

was surprised he'd been listed as her next of kin. Yes, technically they were still married but he never thought of himself as Helen's next of kin.

'He couldn't say too much, but he said it was being treated as a suspected suicide attempt.'

Jack swallowed. His breath caught in his throat. 'Suicide? Christ. Which hospital is she in?' he asked.

'It's called Amager Hospital,' the woman said, clearly reading from her notes.

Jack racked his brains. 'Amager? Where the fuck's that?'

'Copenhagen.'

29

It had been a long time since she had seen Michael looking so vulnerable. Her heart had dropped when he'd told her he needed help. And she wasn't ashamed to admit that her first thought was that he'd played this card before.

She'd tried to help him when he'd ended up in Mildenheath General Hospital after a drugs overdose. She'd brought him home, given him shelter, food and warmth. And how had he repaid her?

She froze on the spot, looking at him lying in his hospital bed. She remembered that night in Robert Ludford's kitchen, strapped to the chair, Michael leaning over her. She felt the fear and dread all over again, the same as she had when he was casually revealing the ways in which he'd killed those five women. But that was due to his mental condition, surely? He was her brother. A boy who'd lost his way. She had to believe that.

You're nothing but a cheap whore! The ultimate cheap whore!

No. He was in a bad place. He was a drug addict. He had mental problems. He needed help. It was a cry for help.

That's all you are, isn't it? Just another little slut. Just the same as you always have been.

A cry for help. That's what it was. He didn't mean any of it. She saw it all the time. Criminals getting caught and flipping out, saying things they didn't mean. They always apologised in the morning once the alcohol had worn off.

You're the next and final one. It's you and then it's me. The world will be rid of all its filth and all its sluts and I will die a hero, a martyr to the cause.

He needed the attention. He'd never had any. He felt hard done by.

I've never felt powerful before, Wend. It's addictive.

It's sorted. Water under the bridge. He's serving his time. He's getting his help. He'll be fine. We'll be fine. He'll be Michael again.

Do you have any last words? Better make them good…

Wendy jumped to her feet, the chair skidding along the hard floor behind her.

She swallowed hard. 'I have to go.'

30

It was starting to feel worryingly familiar to Jack, being at the airport with nothing but his passport and a hastily thrown-together overnight bag. Fortunately for him, Copenhagen was the busiest route from the local airport, with three flights a day leaving for the Danish capital. He was booked on the last, mid-evening flight. As one of the closest capital cities and a centre of European culture, Copenhagen was a popular destination for weekend tourists wanting a quick getaway. For Jack Culverhouse, though, it was going to hold far less pleasant memories, he was sure.

He wondered whether he would have reacted in quite the same way to that phone call had Emily not been back in his life. He'd been quick enough to try to jump on a plane when Antonio García, his contact in the Spanish police, had informed him that he'd found a woman who matched Helen's description over in Spain. But that was because it had been his opportunity to get some answers, some closure. He'd heard neither hide nor hair of her for years, and he needed to know what was going on.

This time, he knew what was going on. He knew Helen was living with borderline personality disorder, that she'd had a number of personal problems involving responsibility and being tied down. She was also a compulsive liar. And now he knew that she'd attempted to take her own life. He remembered the words he was told on the phone: *suspected suicide attempt.* He didn't know if he was just going soft in his old age, but he'd grown to hate the word *suicide* recently. It harked back to a bygone age when it was considered illegal to try to end your own life. In effect, it had been illegal to be ill. It wasn't considered that anyone getting to that stage had been failed by the state, failed by the health service, failed by the system. No, they should be punished for having been so unwell.

He had no doubt about it that he thought differently about Helen now Emily was back in his life. There was a large part of him that despised her for having not only abandoned him, but Emily too. He could forgive her for walking out on him. He was a big boy and could handle that. But walking out on their daughter? That was inexcusable.

He could see a lot of Helen in Emily. The insecurity, the worry, the sense of not quite fitting in with the rest of society. And that worried him. It was up to him now to make sure she had the best possible opportunities in life, but he needed to balance that with not scaring her away at the same time.

Shit. Emily. He hadn't even let her know where he was going. He'd been so wrapped up in his own bloody... He took his phone out of his pocket, unlocked it and called Emily. He didn't know where she'd be. That worried him, but he knew he had to tread carefully when it came to demanding to know every facet of her daily life. That would have scared Helen off, and it'd do the same to Emily too.

He knew he was running a risk by leaving her on her own at her age, but he reckoned he could just about justify that. After all, what other choice did he have? He was going to see Emily's hospitalised mother. He couldn't take her with him, and in any case he'd only be a few hours. He decided to risk it.

'Em? It's me,' he said, when the call connected and Emily answered.

'I know,' Emily replied, her voice a sarcastic sing-song. 'It says on the screen.'

'Yeah. Right. Sorry. Look, something's come up at work and I've got to dash off somewhere overnight. Will you be alright?'

'Yeah, fine,' came Emily's reply.

'You sure? You're not angry?'

'Dad, I think I can deal with turning the lights off myself for one night.'

Culverhouse pursed his lips and nodded to himself. 'Yeah, sorry. Look, I would've let you know earlier if I could, but that's the way these things are sometimes. I'll be back tomorrow, though. Promise,' he said, trying to speak over the sound of the flight departure announcements.

'Are you in an airport?' Emily asked.

'Uh, yeah.'

'Jesus. Where are you going?'

He took half a second to think. Why was Helen in Copenhagen? Did she have some links there? Links Emily would know about?

'Scotland,' he said, holding his voice back. 'Quicker than driving. Got to speak to a witness, but will be back tomorrow.'

'Can't you just phone them?'

'Doesn't work like that unfortunately. When it comes to murder we need to get the statements in person, if we can. Otherwise the defence counsel jump all over it when it comes to court. Can't take that risk.'

'Must be handy being able to see the person, too. You'd know if they were lying,' Emily said.

Culverhouse felt his breath catch. 'Yeah. Yeah, you would.'

'Cool. Well, enjoy. If you can enjoy it, I mean.'

He let out a small chuckle. 'Thanks. I might even treat myself to a small whisky tonight. When in Rome, and all that.'

'See you tomorrow?' Emily said, more as a question than a statement.

'Definitely,' he replied. 'See you tomorrow.'

He'd already resolved not to lie to Emily. If he said he

was going to be back tomorrow, he was going to be back tomorrow. He knew he'd lied to her about where he was going, but that was different; that was to protect her.

He owed it to Emily to visit Helen, to find out what had happened. After all, she was her mother. It was at that point that he realised exactly why he was going to Copenhagen. It certainly wasn't for himself, and it wasn't for Helen either.

31

Wendy couldn't remember a time when she'd felt so tired. Other than the couple of hours' sleep she'd had last night in the Premier Inn in County Durham, she'd been running on empty. The long drive up and the even longer drive back had taken it out of her. It had taken just over five hours to drive back, and she was starting to realise she should have gone straight home.

'There we are. You were wrong,' Steve Wing said to the major incident room as Wendy walked in.

'Sorry?' she replied.

'Frank had twenty quid on this being a mass exodus. We were going to take bets on who'd be next to go AWOL, but you just came back and spoilt it.'

Wendy was, by now, utterly confused. The tiredness wasn't helping matters. 'Sorry, you've lost me, Steve.'

'Well, first of all you disappear off up north and leave the guv to deal with all that, and the next thing we know he's done a runner himself. We thought maybe there was something in the air.'

Steve and Frank chuckled to each other, leaving Wendy none the wiser as to what was going on. 'Done a runner? What do you mean?' she asked. 'Where's he gone?'

DC Ryan Mackenzie answered, looking askance at Steve and Frank as she did so. 'Copenhagen. He had a call to say his wife had tried to end her own life. He's listed as her next of kin, so he's gone over to see her. He's due back on the afternoon flight tomorrow.'

'Christ almighty. And that's what the big fucking joke's all about, is it, Steve?' Wendy shouted, her eyes wide.

Steve seemed to be getting flustered, and looked around himself for support. 'No, I was just—'

'My brother gets beaten to within an inch of his life in prison, and the DCI's wife is so ill that her only way out is to try and top herself, but you fucking idiots see it as the perfect opportunity for a joke and a quick wager. Does that just about cover it?'

Steve Wing looked down at the floor, seemingly well aware that nothing he could say right now would make the situation any better. 'Sorry,' he mumbled.

'Right. And I presume taking the afternoon briefing's going to be down to me as well, then, is it?' Wendy looked around the room and could see there weren't going to be any takers. 'Brilliant. Well, if you don't mind I'm going to delay it until the morning. I'm shattered. In the meantime,

Steve, might I suggest you fuck off for five minutes and get a personality transplant.'

Wendy left the room, a small part of her worried that she was already turning into Jack Culverhouse in his absence. No, she told herself as she jabbed the buttons on the front of the coffee machine. She couldn't blame her foul mood on herself. Not this time. She took the scalding hot cup from the machine and was about to head back towards the incident room when her mobile rang in her pocket. She put the cup down and answered the phone.

'DS Knight? It's Suzanne Corrigan, from the Milden-heath Gazette.'

'Hi Suzanne. Look, can I call you back later? I'm just about to head home.'

'Uh, yeah, you can, but to be honest it'd be much better to chat quickly now if you can.'

Wendy detected some unease in Suzanne's voice. She knew her to be an honest yet forthright journalist. Most people working at the local rag managed the latter fairly well, but tended to struggle when it came to honesty. 'Why, what's up?'

'It's to do with the Hilltop Farm thing,' Suzanne replied. 'We've had the nationals on the phone again. They want to run a piece about it tomorrow.'

Wendy knew damn well that the national newspaper journalists didn't read the Mildenheath Gazette. Most local residents didn't even read it. 'There's nothing to run a piece about,' she said.

'They say they've had more people come forward

about the farm. Stories about stuff having gone on there in the past.'

Wendy's ears pricked up. 'We've had nothing else reported to us,' she said.

'Maybe that's a sign that they don't think the police will believe them. Maybe they don't trust the police.'

Wendy tightened her jaw. 'Well, that's completely irrelevant. If a newspaper runs a story about suspected criminal activity without the police being involved, it could jeopardise the whole thing. We can't have a trial by press, Suzanne.'

'What does it matter? There's not going to be any other sort of trial, is there? Mildenheath Police aren't willing to investigate.'

Wendy tried to keep hold of her temper. 'It's not a case of not being willing, Suzanne. It's a case of not having been presented with any evidence of any crimes having been committed. Anonymous tip-offs and rumour-mill stories aren't enough to charge.'

'They're going to print in the morning,' Suzanne said, changing her tone of voice completely.

'Right. Well we've got nothing more to add,' Wendy replied.

'What about a quote from DCI Culverhouse? Even if it says there's nothing more to add. We just need something for balance.'

'Suzanne, leave it. I'll get him to call you when he gets back.'

There was a moment of silence on the other end of the line. 'When's that going to be?' Suzanne asked.

'His flight's due in tomorrow afternoon,' Wendy said, without thinking. 'Now, I really have to go.'

She ended the call, thrust her mobile phone back into her pocket and downed the cup of coffee. She could see exactly where Suzanne Corrigan was coming from. She felt the same way. Why wasn't more being done about the reports at Hilltop Farm? Accusations of heavy-handedness were one thing, but they were nothing compared to the shitstorm that would occur if it transpired that the reports were true, and had been more or less ignored by the police.

Either way, Wendy was convinced there was more to Hilltop Farm than met the eye. And while she had some say, she was determined to get to the bottom of it.

32

The drive from Copenhagen Airport to Amager Hospital took just under ten minutes — far longer than it had taken for him to get off the plane, go through Customs and find a taxi. The route was scenic, and one he'd like to take by day sometime, in happier circumstances.

Just outside the airport, they passed under the famous Øresund Bridge. The bridge linked Denmark to Sweden at Mälmo, just before it dipped its nose under the water, the lights disappearing beneath the Øresund Strait before reappearing five miles later on the artificial island of Peber-holm. Although Jack didn't watch much TV himself, he'd heard his colleagues talking about the Scandinavian crime series *The Bridge*, which was set in the area. It was just another name on the long list of TV programmes and films he'd resolved to watch one day but knew he probably never would.

They continued up the road towards the hospital, the

shoreline hugging their right-hand side. Within a minute or two they were out in what looked like a rural area, with nothing but the lights of oncoming cars. Another minute and they were back in civilisation, in an area that looked as though it could be any small European town. They were in the suburbs, he knew that much.

Turning left off the main road, they passed some small houses in what could have been mistaken for a British housing estate. Jack noted the streetlights that dangled over the road, suspended by wires and cables running between the buildings.

The taxi pulled up at a jaunty angle near the impressive-looking hospital building. There was nothing that screamed the fact that it was a hospital. On any other day he was quite sure he would've walked straight past it without even realising. It looked more like a stately home. He paid the driver and made his way through the car park to the imposing-looking front door. The name AMAGER HOSPITAL was emblazoned across the top of it in brass lettering. The studded wooden door looked more like the entrance to a psychiatric institution than a general hospital. And, just for a moment, Jack wondered whether he'd been fed the right information. Had something been lost in translation?

Inside, it looked every inch a hospital. He wandered through the corridors, the building looking about as busy as he could expect it to be for that time of night. He tried to make sense of the signs, which were, of course, written in Danish. After a few minutes of wandering, he found a manned reception desk. He asked the woman sitting behind it where he needed to go for the Accident & Emergency department. The woman explained he was in the wrong area of the building and needed to follow signs for *Akutmodtagelse* — a word he forgot as soon as he'd seen it, but noted the distinctive red cross symbol.

When he finally got there, he was impressed by the speed at which he was taken to Helen. He'd half expected to be told that he'd have to wait until visiting hours. The doctor who met him was a slim man, with short grey hair and rimmed glasses. He spoke in a soft accent that told Jack that although he was Danish, he'd spent a lot of time in either England or — judging by the pronunciation of certain words — America.

'You made good time,' the doctor said, looking at his watch. 'The joys of air travel, eh? Now, how much were you told on the phone?'

'Not much, to be honest,' Jack replied. 'Just that she'd tried to kill herself. The message was passed on to me by somebody else. I was at work.'

The doctor's voice was calm and easy. 'Yes, she was found by some Canadian tourists on a park bench on Øresundsvej, just north of here. We call it Lergravsparken — the clay pit park. She had a note in her pocket which gave you as the next of kin.'

Jack's head was spinning. What was she even doing here in Denmark? Why had she wanted to end her life? Why had she been so keen for Jack to be the one to have to deal with the fallout? 'What happened?' he asked.

'The signs look like an overdose of prescription painkillers. Perhaps a tranquilliser of some sort, but we'll know when the test results are back. She was extremely pale, her breathing was remarkably shallow and she seemed to be unable to speak. To anyone else she would have looked drunk, but the couple who found her were both medical students. They recognised the nystagmus, the uncontrolled rapid movement of the eyes. Most drunk people would have slow, lazy eye movements. Your wife's eyes were quite the opposite. It's a stroke of luck that this couple found her, as anyone else might have left her and ignored her as a drunk.'

'But what was she doing there?' Jack asked, struggling to take in all this information at once. 'I mean, does she live here?'

The doctor shrugged. 'Your guess is as good as mine. I don't know her.'

Neither do I, Jack wanted to say. 'And is she alright? I mean, will she be alright?'

'She's stable,' the doctor said, nodding slowly. 'But we won't know what damage has been done until we can run some further tests. For now, it's important that she rests. She's had a gastric irrigation and I imagine she'll be in some pain from that.'

'A gastric irrigation?' Jack asked. 'You mean a stomach pump?'

'Yes, a stomach pump. It's not a particularly pleasant procedure, but it gets the drugs out of her stomach quickly.'

Jack nodded. He knew Helen was troubled, but to go to this extent was truly shocking.

'Do you have any other questions?' the doctor asked.

Culverhouse took a deep breath before answering. 'Yes. Can I see her?'

33

Wendy had a feeling that the morning briefing was going to be far more eventful than it otherwise might have been. Debbie Weston alerted her to the newspaper reports on Hilltop Farm at five-thirty that morning. Debbie had always been an early bird, but Wendy was agog at how she could get up at that time of the morning just to go out and get a newspaper. Especially with the stress and long, tiring hours of this job.

Wendy had taken a few minutes to read through the article and note the gist of it before the briefing. Her overriding feeling was that she was keen for the team to spring into action as fast as possible — whatever that action might end up being.

'Right. I presume everyone's read the article in the paper today?' Wendy said, opening the morning briefing. She was met by a succession of nods and murmurs. 'Good. Now, we're in a position where we can't win. We're damned if we do, and we're damned if we don't. If we ignore this completely we'll look incompetent. Particularly if it turns out something untoward *is* going on at Hilltop Farm. And if we go in all guns blazing right now we're on a hiding to nothing. We'll either look reactionary after the media coverage or daft if we go in and find nothing.'

There was a moment of silence as Wendy let that settle in.

'So what do you want us to do?' Frank Vine asked, from the back of the room.

If Wendy was completely honest, she didn't have a clue. She was completely out of her depth. Most investigations began with some hard evidence of some sort. There would at least be evidence that someone had committed a crime, even if the rest of the details were scarce. This time, though, she was going purely on a hunch. She was sure that some crimes had been committed at Hilltop Farm, but she was unable to get much further than that.

A police officer's hunch could be a double-edged sword. It could lead you to probe in areas that other people wouldn't even think of. But at the same time it had the disadvantage of allowing you to remain blind to everything else if you got too bogged down with a preconceived idea of what had happened. Wendy, though, tended to trust her hunches. They hadn't failed her too often in the past — at least not in her professional life.

'That's the problem, Frank,' she said. 'I'm not entirely sure at this stage. But let's look at the facts. The newspaper reports are that people are being held there against their will. Some are perhaps being assaulted or abused on occasion, and there was the anonymous phone call reporting that someone had died there. The paper claims they've got a "number" of people who used to be members of the cult and who have come forward to blow the whistle. We need to get those names. Debbie, can you put in a call?'

Debbie Weston nodded.

Wendy could feel herself getting fired up. She was on a roll. 'Even if it does turn out to all be horse shit, the fact remains that these people have now made serious allegations and we need to investigate them. With any luck, there'll be enough grounds to enable us to go in and do a full-on search of the farm. Finances, records, taking people in for questioning, the lot. But we need more than just anonymous reports of a dead body somewhere on the farm. We need dates, exact locations, names of people involved. Something we can use. Get those names and addresses of the people who came forward to the newspaper and we'll go and speak to them.'

Now she was starting to realise that Suzanne Corrigan's interference could have actually thrown them a lifeline. 'In fact, I'll do that. I'll get the call in. In the meantime, I want the rest of you to clear your schedules and prepare. With any luck, we're going to have a busy few days ahead of us.'

Steve Wing shuffled uncomfortably in his seat before speaking. 'Uh, in that case, shouldn't someone call the DCI?'

34

Jack had sat next to Helen for most of the night, watching her sleep and recover not only from her overdose but the resulting stomach pump. She looked as though she could sleep for days.

A succession of nurses had come in throughout the night to check on her and jot down her blood pressure, heart rate and various other vital signs. The doctors had told him it would take a good few days — if not longer — for Helen to recover. Those were a good few days Jack didn't have. He had his return flight booked for this afternoon. He'd booked it at the same time as his outbound flight, knowing that he needed to commit to it to keep his promise to Emily. He had to be back today, come what may.

Around ten-thirty that morning, Danish time, Helen started to stir. He noticed her face starting to move slightly — micromovements — followed by a strange groaning sound. Once the doctors had checked her over and were satisfied that she was still stable, they left the two of them together.

'Jack. What are you doing here?' Helen said, her voice dry and rasping.

'I was hoping you could tell me that. They found my contact details on you, listed as your next of kin. They reckon you carried them on purpose, wanted me to be called.'

Helen blinked a couple of times and swallowed. 'What — what happened?'

'They don't know. A couple of Canadian medical students found you in a park. They reckon you overdosed on tranquillisers.'

Helen didn't respond to this. In Jack's eyes, she knew damn well what had happened. More likely, she wanted to know either what the hospital had presumed about the circumstances or what Jack was willing to tell her. He had half a mind, too, that she was trying to judge his reactions and emotions. Ever the consummate professional, Jack kept emotion out of his voice as best he could. 'Do you want to tell me what this is all about?' he asked.

She seemed to think about this for a few moments before speaking. 'Tell me it wouldn't be better for everyone if I wasn't around.'

'It'd certainly make life a lot easier at times,' he replied, exhaling. 'But I don't think that's the best option overall, no.'

'I don't think there is any other option,' she whispered.

Jack looked her in the eye, feeling somewhat sorry for her, but mostly just frustrated. 'So you don't think you're able to get better at all? With medication, therapy, stability, the support of your family?'

Helen turned her head away and looked towards the window. 'What family,' she said, more as a statement than a question.

'Emily. Your parents. Me. As much as you might not like it, we're still married. I still have a responsibility to care for you. And I'm not being funny, but none of us have ever gone anywhere. We've always stayed exactly where we are, willing to help you. No-one asked you to leave all those years ago. No-one asked you to dump Emily at your parents'. No-one sent you off to sodding Copenhagen. We're all here, trying to do our bit, but you keep running away from us.'

'I'm not running away from any of you,' she whispered. 'I'm running away from myself, from my stupid actions.'

'And you think I don't know that? I get it, Helen. Trust me, I really do. But this isn't the way to deal with things. This isn't helping anyone, least of all you.' He sensed he wasn't going to get a response and realised there was no use in trying to flog a dead horse. 'Emily got in touch with me,' he said, trying to steer the conversation towards more hopeful topics. He saw some movement on Helen's face, and she turned her head towards him as he spoke. 'I don't think she's having a great time with your parents. She's been staying at mine for a bit. Just until school starts back, I mean. We'll have to sort something out by then. She's looking well. She's turning out to be a great kid.' Jack hated lying to his wife while she was in this state, but she at least needed something to cling onto.

'How?' Helen asked. It was a word that didn't say much, but Jack understood it to mean a thousand words.

'Honestly? I tracked her down. Well, I had some help. She wasn't exactly over the moon to see me at first, but I left my number with her and she called me. She didn't really remember the house or where it was, as you'd expect. She was young when she left. But she seems to be settling in alright. She's spoken to your parents about it. I think they understand.' He omitted to mention the fact that he'd not spoken to his in-laws since the day Helen left, and that he only had Emily's word for it that she'd told them where she was staying. If she hadn't, she would have been reported missing long before now.

There was one question Jack was desperate to ask his wife. One he'd tried asking her before, but to which she hadn't given a proper answer. It was an answer he needed to hear. 'When did you last see her?' he finally asked.

Helen's face looked pained. 'Honestly? I don't know. It was in a supermarket somewhere. We didn't speak. She didn't see me. But I knew it was her straight away. My parents didn't see me either. I managed to keep out of the way. I didn't want any of them seeing me like... like that.'

Even though Helen didn't explain what she meant, Jack knew. She'd either been going through a dark patch, was high on prescription drugs or had been drunk. He knew his wife well enough to know that at least one of the three would be going on at any given time.

Jack looked at his watch. 'Look, I've got a couple more hours but I have to fly back this afternoon. I've got some bits I need to sort out. But I can come back over. We can get you well, get you home and start to work through this all together. Alright? You've got my support, and I'm sure you've got Emily's support too.'

Before he could say anything else, he was interrupted by the sound of his phone ringing. He'd switched it on half an hour or so earlier, when he'd popped outside for some fresh air. It had been off all night, and he realised it should probably be on in case work needed to get hold of him.

'Culverhouse,' he said, not looking at the display as he answered the call. He recognised the voice of Wendy Knight straight away, and listened as she told him exactly what he didn't want to hear.

35

Ben Gallagher knew they needed more. He'd sent out another message to his brother. He hoped the drone had come over as planned the night before, to read the message he'd chalked on the rooftop herb garden. But even so, that call to arms wasn't going to be enough. It would make Harry realise how serious and immediate the situation was. But convincing Harry had never been the aim. It was the police they needed to convince, and that was proving to be a whole lot more difficult.

The trouble was, Ben knew what had been going on. He'd been feeding that information out through his brother, but they needed more than that. They needed proof. They needed evidence. And there was only one way they were ever going to be able to get that evidence: Ben had to get it himself.

He was sure that Amy Kemp must still be inside the medical centre, whether dead or alive. His living quarters were closest to the medical centre. He knew he would've heard someone moving a body in or out of there. He couldn't be certain, but he was pretty sure. Either way, there must be some sort of evidence there — something he could find which would help him to blow the whole place apart.

His only worry was how he was going to do it. Creeping around in the dead of night would be one thing, but the farm was deathly dark at night. There was no way he'd be able to get in there without some sort of help in the form of light. Light that other people would be able to see. Light that Father Joseph's henchmen would see. Any sort of noise at night would be spotted straightaway as suspicious, too. That only left one possibility: He had to go in during the day. And there was no better time than the present.

He stood up and smoothed down his shirt with his hands. Taking a deep breath, he pushed open the door and squinted as the bright light of the day streamed in and hit him square in the face. He raised his hand to his forehead, blocking out the worst of it as his eyes adjusted, closed the door behind him and allowed himself to breathe calmly.

The sound of his footsteps on the ground seemed louder and crunchier than usual, mixed with the deep thudding bass of the blood pulsing at his eardrums. Everything seemed far more vivid, far more real. His skin felt hypersensitive and he swore he could taste the inside of his mouth. The short walk to the medical centre seemed to take much longer than usual, too, as if time had slowed down. Everything seemed to be accentuated.

When he finally got there, after what seemed like an age, he considered for the first time what he was actually going to do. He hadn't thought that far ahead. On the face of it, there wasn't much thinking ahead he could do: he had no idea what he should expect when he got inside. All he knew was that he needed to find some evidence of what had happened to Amy Kemp, but he had no idea what that evidence might be.

He put out his hand and pushed at the front door. Worth a shot, he thought. To his disbelief, the door began to swing open, creaking on its hinges as it did so. He stood for a moment, half-expecting something dramatic to happen. When nothing did happen, he stepped inside. He gave his eyes a chance to adjust to the relative darkness inside, and closed the door behind him. He half-felt his way through the dark, stone corridor. At the end, on the right, was an opening into a large space that could — at a stretch — be called a room.

He took a step into the room and followed the stream of light from the high latticed window as it lit up a square section of the stone floor. Just behind it, huddled against the wall, was Amy Kemp. She was alive — he could see that much from her chest heaving. But she didn't look as though she was in a particularly bright condition.

He walked over towards her, hoping that she might recognise him and realise she was safe. As he got there, Amy opened her eyes and looked at him. The whites of her eyes were yellow and weak. She opened her mouth to speak but no sound came out.

Ben leaned forward slightly to try and hear what she was saying. He could just about make out one or two words. It was only at the moment he realised those words were *behind you* that he felt the crushing blow connect with his skull.

36

Jack had always hated waiting around in airports. That was one of the reasons why he was one of those people who only turned up for their flight with half an hour to spare. Just enough time to get through security, have a quick piss and jump on the plane. This time, though, he'd got to Copenhagen Airport much earlier than necessary. It was as if just being at the airport would make the plane leave quicker. Following Wendy's phone call, he wasn't sure it could come quickly enough.

He hadn't given Hilltop Farm a second thought, save for the chat he'd had with the Chief Constable about it. He was convinced there was nothing untoward going on there. Sure, they were a bunch of freakish hippies and religious loons, but there was nothing illegal about that. Nothing he needed to get involved with. But on hearing about the other reports that had been made in the national papers, it was clear to him that something must be going on. After all, there could be no smoke without fire. And there was an awful fucking lot of smoke coming out of Hilltop Farm right about now.

Wendy had let him know that they were onto the newspaper to get a list of names and addresses for the informants. They'd split up into teams to interview them, with Jack due to meet Frank Vine back at the station on his return. Together, they'd speak to one of the informants on the list and see what might come from that.

He knew the pattern all too well. One person would make a report about something that seemed ludicrous, and no evidence would be found. But once that story got out, others would come forward and the allegations would have a lot more credibility. One snowflake can't break a tree branch, but a build up of snowflakes makes an avalanche. He'd seen it happen many times. Policing in the UK had been rocked to the core in recent years. The claims about politicians, entertainers and celebrities abusing young children had seemed ludicrous at first. But when the real extent of the culture of abuse perpetuated by people like Jimmy Savile had come to light, it seemed incredible that it was ever covered up. Sometimes, the most preposterous and magnificent claims and theories were the ones that were right. And they were the ones that were least likely ever to be investigated, purely because of their presumed absurdity.

He'd had all this — and more — on his mind as he waited for the almost two-hour flight home. On any other occasion, he would've bought a newspaper and read that to pass the time. But that wasn't an option today. He'd find himself getting frustrated by reading about how inept they thought his force was. Either that or he'd end up allowing the newspaper articles to inform his judgement before he'd even got his teeth into the case. Neither option would be ideal.

Instead, he sat in silence and gazed out of the window as the plane skipped over the northern tip of Germany and soared over the North Sea. Lost in his thoughts, the flight didn't seem to take as long as he expected. Before he knew it, he was tugging his bag out of the overhead locker and squeezing himself down the aisle to the front door of the plane.

His thoughts turned to Emily as he queued at Passport Control. He'd have to try and make the interview with the informant as quick as he could. He'd promised Emily he'd be back late afternoon, early evening. And he knew he couldn't break that promise. He'd broken enough in the past.

Once he was through security, he followed the snaking corridor round towards the main terminal exit. He dodged the wheelie suitcases and slow-walking pensioners with their trolleys and got to the main arrivals hall. As he came through the archway, he clocked the waiting relatives and taxi drivers with surnames written on bits of card. Before he could register anything else, he was taken aback by the sound of a woman calling his name.

'DCI Culverhouse, do you have a moment?'

Just as he was about to answer, a man came up the other side of him with a microphone.

'Can you comment on the allegations about potential murders and abuse at Hilltop Farm?'

'Do you think it's acceptable to go on holiday while you're in charge of a major investigation?' another voice asked as a flashbulb went off in front of his face.

Before long, the voices all merged into one, building to a crescendo.

'Were you on holiday?'

'Would you say you fiddled while Rome burned?'

'Who's in charge of the investigation now?'

Ducking and avoiding the journalists, photographers and interviewers, Jack side-stepped into the toilets. He shoved his hand into his pocket to find a twenty-pence piece for the barrier. Without looking behind him, he headed straight for the cubicle on the far end of the gents'. He pushed open the door and locked it behind him.

He leaned back against the door and let his body slide down it. His chest heaved with silent sobs as he buried his head in his hands.

37

It had taken far too long for Wendy to convince the national newspaper to hand over their list of informants. They had many excuses, but she suspected the primary one was pure spite. Initially, they'd trotted out their usual 'duty to protect our informants' line. She'd rebutted that with her usual 'illegal to knowingly hinder an active police investigation' response. It was the usual merry dance, and one she'd seen many times in the past. When she'd finally convinced them they'd have to hand over the information, they'd pushed everything back to square one by pointing out that Wendy was a mere Detective Sergeant. They could only consider a request from a Senior Investigating Officer of at least Detective Inspector rank, they said. With Culverhouse AWOL, that had meant a call to Malcolm Pope.

Malcolm Pope was a man universally despised within

Mildenheath CID. Fortunately for them, he was based twenty-odd miles away at Milton House, the county's police headquarters. He'd long been a thorn in the side of Jack Culverhouse, always pushing for the final amalgamation of Mildenheath CID into county HQ. Mildenheath had — so far — stemmed the tide, bucked the trend. But Malcolm Pope was more than keen to see Culverhouse's unit brought under his wing, leaving him to rule over the county's CID roost. Mildenheath CID's success rate, the town's serious crime rate and the ageing Chief Constable's dislike of mergers, though, had enabled the status quo to remain. For now.

Pope had, of course, taken a couple of hours to comb through all the information and consider Wendy's request. She knew damn well that if one of his own Detective Sergeants had put a form on his desk and asked him to sign it, he would've done it blindfolded. But when the request came from someone at Mildenheath, there were games that could be played.

It was four o'clock in the afternoon by the time Wendy had a list of three names and addresses. By then, the team had managed to formulate the questions they wanted to ask each of them. Wendy had decided that she and Ryan Mackenzie would visit one, Steve Wing and Debbie Weston another and Frank Vine was to wait for Culverhouse to return before the pair visited the third.

The three informants were all people whose families were still living at Hilltop Farm. They had been keen to keep their anonymity in the newspaper article, and would likely be shocked when the police came knocking. For that reason, they'd decided not to call ahead and spook anyone, but to just turn up at their doors. When dealing with people who'd spent a lifetime being petrified of authority figures, it was best not to allow them the chance to disappear.

Wendy and Ryan drove the sixty miles to the home of Sandra Kaporsky. Sandra was a woman in her fifties who'd been working as a missionary, or recruiter, for the church before deciding to abscond. The newspaper article had detailed how the missionaries were the only people who'd be allowed to enter and leave the farm almost of their own accord, as was necessitated by their role in recruiting new members and bringing them to live on the farm. Because of that, the recruiters tended to be the more hardline, dedicated members of the church. It wasn't a role that was given to just anyone, but instead was handed to people who'd displayed their true devotion to the church. Wendy realised that would mean Sandra must have had furthest to fall in terms of losing her faith in the church, so she wanted to visit her personally.

Sandra's house was small and unassuming, a mid-terrace house nestled in a street of many other similar houses. Wendy supposed that Sandra wouldn't have had much money on leaving the church, so it was pretty impressive that she had a roof over her head at all.

A few seconds after they knocked on the door, it opened and a meek-looking woman answered it.

'Sandra Kaporsky? I'm DS Wendy Knight and this is DC Ryan Mackenzie, from Mildenheath Police. We're here because we think you might be able to help us with an investigation into Hilltop Farm.' She noticed that Sandra still seemed a little unsure. 'Here are our ID cards. Feel free to ring 101 and verify them first of all. We want to make sure you feel completely comfortable.'

Sandra looked at the cards and shook her head before opening the door to let them in.

They weren't offered tea or coffee. To Wendy's mind, Sandra seemed to be pretty shaken up and nervous. She wondered what the poor woman had been through in her life. To live in perpetual fear of a group of people must eat away at you over time.

'First things first, Sandra. You aren't in any trouble at all. We actually need your help. We've been looking into Hilltop Farm for quite some time now,' she lied, 'and we keep hitting brick walls. When we saw the newspaper article we realised there were people out there with information. Information that could maybe lead to arrests and even convictions.' She left that hanging in the air for a few moments, not expecting Sandra to say much back, if anything.

'I told the reporter everything,' Sandra said, almost whispering, her voice quivering.

'I know, but we need to get it for our records, I'm afraid. I know it's not nice going over things again, but we need an official statement.'

Sandra nodded ever so slightly.

'Now, there are a few comments and allegations in the article that I'll want to ask you about. But for now I think it's probably best if you tell your story in your own words. We want you to feel comfortable and go at your own pace.'

Sandra shuffled in her seat, swallowing hard before she began to speak. 'I joined the church at fifteen. I didn't do well at school. Nowadays they'd probably call it dyslexia or something, but back then you were just thick. My parents were so disappointed. They were both doctors. GPs. So I left home and joined the church. I think they were both too work-driven to even notice. The church gave me a home, a purpose. I gained confidence, got an identity. At least I thought I did. After a while I became a recruiter. Our job was to go out and find people who'd be willing to come and join the church. The way they told me everything seemed so normal, but now when I look back it was just wrong.'

'How do you mean?' Wendy asked.

'I mean things like the sorts of people we were meant to approach. We're talking homeless people, runaway kids, people in a fragile mental state. It was framed that we would be helping these people and showing them that God gives everyone a second chance. But looking back now it's obvious they were just vulnerable people. Put it this way: they didn't get many successful businessmen or architects to join the church.'

Wendy nodded at Ryan, indicating that she should feel free to ask a question.

'And what was life on the farm like?' Ryan asked. 'From day to day, I mean.'

Sandra's eyes seemed to drift off to a faraway place. 'Different,' she said, eventually. 'At first it seemed great. It was like *The Good Life*, you know? That TV series. It was all self-sufficiency, going back to our roots, just us and the community and God. All the confusion and extra layers of life were gone. It was simple. Satisfyingly simple.'

'And did it stay like that?' Ryan asked.

Sandra shook her head and smiled. 'No. Well, yes, it did, but that was the problem. It was missing so much. It was missing soul. And sometimes... Sometimes things happen that can strip the soul out of anything.'

'What sort of things?'

'Bad things. Sorry, do you mind if I take a moment?' Sandra asked, her voice starting to crack.

Wendy nodded and gestured that it was fine, and Sandra rose and walked through to the kitchen. Wendy and Ryan shared a look as they heard the noise of Sandra blowing her nose. There were a few moments of silence before Sandra came back into the room, sat down and took a deep breath.

'Nice photo,' Wendy said, gesturing to a picture on the mantelpiece. It showed Sandra, probably only a couple of years ago, and a large German Shepherd dog. They were standing on top of a rocky cliff-face, tufts of grass teasing up around her ankles.

'Yes,' Sandra said, smiling slightly. 'That's down near Lulworth Cove, on the Jurassic Coast. I go down there sometimes when I need to clear my head. That's Docker, my friend's dog. They run a café a little further along the coast. They let me take him out for walks when I'm down there.'

'Lovely part of the country,' Wendy said. She could see Sandra's mind shifting back to the original topic of conversation. Her face seemed to darken slightly as she spoke without prompting.

'It was a Sunday. I remember that much. I remember thinking that it was the holy day. I mean, in that church all the days are holy, but there's still something special about a Sunday. There was a strange car sitting opposite the front gates to the farm. There wasn't anyone in it, but it's not the sort of place where you park a car. It's just a massive long grass verge, then hedges and fields. There's literally nothing else around there but the farm. It didn't seem right, so I went to report it.' Wendy noticed Sandra swallowing before she continued to speak. 'I went to knock on the door, and just before I did I heard a noise. It sounded like a whimpering sort of noise, but sharper. I can't describe it, but I can still hear it now. Something didn't seem right, so I walked away from the door and peered in through the corner of the window. And I —' Sandra stopped speaking, her voice catching.

'It's okay,' Wendy said, putting her hand on Sandra's arm. 'Take your time.'

'I saw Father Joseph, on top of a young girl. She must have been maybe ten or eleven at most. And in that moment everything just fell apart. It was like a veil falling from in front of my eyes, taking my faith with it. Everything I believed, everything I knew. It was just gone.'

Wendy looked at Ryan. This was a story they hadn't been aware of until now. The newspaper article had mentioned 'allegations of abuse', but this was far more serious than either of them had anticipated.

'Did you tell anyone about this at the time?' Wendy asked.

Sandra almost laughed. 'Like who? When you realise the person right at the top is the one doing these things, who can you go to? Everything leads up to him. There is nowhere to go, nowhere to run. But I knew I couldn't stay there. The next day, when I went out to speak to a potential recruit, I kept walking and didn't come back.'

'Do you know who the girl was?' Ryan asked.

Sandra shook her head. 'No. I hadn't seen her before and I haven't seen her since.'

'And did you tell anyone on the outside?'

'No. Definitely not. That's what you need to understand. These people, they're everywhere. You think they're just inside Hilltop Farm, they're not. They're on the outside too, trying to pull people in. They're the recruiters, they're the watchers.'

'Watchers?' Wendy asked.

'They watch all the time. You're never free of them.'

'Are they watching you now?' Wendy was starting to become concerned.

'No. I changed my name, changed my appearance. Sandra isn't the name I had on the farm. It's not the name I was born with. Up until now I've managed. But I know that one day, any day, they could find me. And I know that day would be my last.'

'How do you mean?' Wendy asked.

'They're dangerous people. More than dangerous. If they found me, they'd kill me. I know that for a fact. I know too much. And now that it's all in the papers, and with the police... Oh God. I don't know what they'll do.'

38

By the time the team had assembled back at the major incident room at Mildenheath CID later that evening, everyone was flagging. Jack Culverhouse was flagging more than most, having stepped straight off his flight from Copenhagen and gone with Frank Vine to visit one of the former residents of Hilltop Farm. Now, having barely had time to pause at the coffee machine on the way past, he was starting — and hopefully before long ending — the evening briefing. With any luck, he'd be able to get home for a bit shortly and hope that Emily hadn't already upped and left.

'First things first, Frank and I went to visit a man by the name of Richard Smale. He says his wife and children were convinced to join the church at Hilltop Farm — or rather his wife was, and she took the kids with her. They tried to convince him too, but he wasn't having it. He reckons he's spent the past few years being tracked and bugged by people involved with the church. Within a month his already-fragile business started haemorrhaging clients. Friends had stopped speaking to him and he kept finding odd messages waiting for him at home and at work. In the end he got so paranoid he moved away and started afresh.'

'Is there anything that can link that to Hilltop Farm, though?' Ryan Mackenzie asked.

Culverhouse gave her a cold, hard stare. 'That's what we intend to find out, DC Mackenzie. That's our job. Now, his kids will be about eight and thirteen now. Both girls. He's worried about them being brought up in that sort of community at an impressionable age. When he saw the local newspaper reports online about the body and our original search, it compelled him to get the ball rolling. Why he called a newspaper and not the police is anyone's fucking guess, but there you go. Knight?'

Wendy stood up, not having expected him to be handing over to her quite so soon. 'Uh, yeah. That kind of ties in to what we found out, too. We spoke to a woman called Sandra Kaporsky — not her original name. She used to be a recruiter for the church. She has a similar view to Richard Smale with regards to people from the church being powerful and having influence out in the wider community. Again, nothing that we can pin down, so it might just be that the church has managed to fuel their paranoia. But the most disturbing thing was that she mentioned witnessing a sexual assault, possibly a rape, on a young girl.'

'How young?' Culverhouse asked.

'Ten or eleven, she thinks.'

'Fuck.'

'That in itself gives us grounds for arresting Father Joseph Kümmel,' Wendy said. 'We'll also be able to search for and seize evidence.'

'Good work. Steve and Debbie?'

'A man called James Aston,' Steve said. 'Again, like Sandra, he changed his name when he left Hilltop Farm. His family are still at the farm. He mentioned particularly his brother, Ben. James's original name was Harry Gallagher. He told us his brother has been sending out secret messages by writing them in chalk on the top of a building. James — Harry — has been reading the messages using a drone camera. All pretty clever stuff, but a miracle they haven't been caught to be honest with you. That's not all, though. When we asked him why he hadn't reported any of what Ben had told him to the police, he said he had. He clammed up a bit then, but we finally managed to get to the bottom of it. He admitted that it was him who made the anonymous phone call about the body.'

'Brilliant. Really fucking excellent, Steve. Nice one,' Culverhouse said, clenching his fists. There was a definite air of confidence in the room, with the whole team feeling they might finally be onto something. With three pretty solid witnesses and some concrete allegations, they'd be able to bring Father Joseph Kümmel in for questioning. They could also start a proper, full search of the farm and its records. 'Right. As I see it we have two duties now. One is to make sure we provide protection to our witnesses. More than one of them has raised fears about being watched. We can't risk anything happening to any of them. Debbie, can you arrange for uniformed officers to keep an eye on the three houses? Particularly while we've got Father Joseph Kümmel in for questioning. I'll get authorisation to go in and arrest Kümmel. We're going to need plenty of numbers, as we need to take them by surprise. We don't want anyone trying to hide evidence or burn records. Not that they won't have done already with the forewarning they had a few days ago. In the meantime,' Jack said, looking at his watch, 'I'm going home for a few hours and I think you all should too. With any luck the authorisation will be given in the next few hours. As soon as it is, we're going in. I'm aiming for early hours of the morning, if not sooner. We don't have time to waste.'

The team nodded their assent, thankful that they might at least get a couple of hours' sleep. With the anticipation of what was to come, though, there was little chance of sleep being at the forefront of any of their minds.

39

For Father Joseph Kümmel, the time had come. He didn't feel sad; he knew from the moment he started the church that there was only going to be one way it could end.

Since day one, he had been in full control. And even recently, when that control had started to slip, he was able to rein it back in and remain in charge. The foundations had been laid long ago, and reinforced regularly ever since. He had long suspected that religion was the purest form of ancient psychology, centuries before the term had even been coined. And that theory had been put into practise, beautifully and perfectly.

He'd had his theory proven early on, when he read the news reports from the Peoples Temple in Jonestown, Guyana. There'd been a small tinge of regret at first that Jim Jones had got there before him, but it was all for the greater good. He couldn't deny it had made his job far more difficult, especially while Jonestown was still fresh in the mind for many. But there were always going to be enough desperate suckers in the world.

He'd go out with a bang. They all would. It was the only way it was ever going to end. He wasn't deluded enough to believe that he'd be lauded as a revolutionary hero. Not straight away, anyway. But he would be used as a case study for decades to come. The psychology — the long-game — was sublime. The story of Hilltop Farm would hit the national and international news outlets, of course, but he'd also be cited in psychology textbooks. He'd spark debates over religion and could even start a revolution from beyond the grave. No-one ever knows what impact their death will have on the world, but he could be pretty sure that the deaths of the entire community at Hilltop Farm would have a big one.

The endgame hadn't been designed at first. Not in detail, anyway. But Jim Jones had done it to perfection. Cyanide. Why hadn't he thought of that before? It seemed so logical afterwards. The human body killing itself, turning in on itself. Gulping down the oxygen but refusing to use it. Their lungs would be unaffected. They could breathe all they wanted. But their red blood cells would refuse to take the oxygen. Even with all the will in the world, they still wouldn't be in control of their own bodies. It was poetic. And when he considered the possibility of them deliberately taking the cyanide, and forcing that complete helplessness and lack of control on themselves, he realised the plan was perfect.

Creating the cyanide over time hadn't been as difficult

as he'd thought. For one of the deadliest substances on the planet, it was pretty easy to make. Coal, ammonia and sodium gave them hydrogen cyanide, which was then treated with sodium hydroxide — caustic soda. The exact method and science was lost on him, but he hadn't needed to know the details. That was for people far cleverer than him to worry about.

He'd been encouraged by the reaction to his sermon. The thought of the outside world encroaching on Hilltop Farm and coming to break up the community was anathema to everything the parishioners had worked for. They'd given up the lives they'd been born into, some had left their families. All had dedicated years to the cause, to working for complete freedom and dedication to God. There was only one way they could react when forced into a corner. The only way to keep their freedom and show their dedication to the church and to God was to act in the way Father Joseph wanted them to. The way God had told them to. And it would complete the circle, would bring the long story of Hilltop Farm to a perfect, poetic close.

It was meant to be.

It would happen tomorrow. It felt right. He'd expected he might be nervous, excited, but he wasn't. He was calm, almost serene. It was a feeling of complete acceptance that the moment had come. It was to be his final act.

He stood, looked at himself in the mirror and saw a version of himself fifty years younger.

Yes. It had all come full circle.

It was beautiful.

40

Jack knew he wouldn't be getting much sleep. But even the slightest possibility of catching forty winks right now was all that was keeping him going. He'd have to keep his mobile phone with him at all times, knowing that he could receive a call at any moment. When the call came, he'd have to be able to spring into action immediately.

When he got home, Emily had been sitting in the living room, watching TV. Ordinarily, he would've balked at the thought of a kid of her age being up so late, watching the sort of stuff that was on the screens at this time of night. But he knew he had to give her some leeway. After all, he'd not exactly been present recently. Besides which, Emily had been extraordinarily understanding, especially considering Jack's track record.

'Alright?' he said, trying to be as casual as possible without looking as though he was completely unaware of his transgressions.

'Yeah, fine.'

'Sorry I'm late.'

'It's cool, don't worry. Did you catch them?' Emily asked.

'Catch who?'

'The bad guys,' she replied, a cheeky smile playing across her face. It was a smile he hadn't seen for years.

Jack chuckled. 'Not yet. But we're close. We'll be picking them up in the early hours of the morning, with any luck.'

Emily nodded. 'Will you have to go in?'

'Yeah. Probably,' he replied. 'Sorry.'

'Honestly. It's cool. I don't mind having a bit of space to myself. It's better than... Well, it's better than being at Nan and Grandad's.'

Jack sensed that she might be willing to tell him a bit more about why she didn't want to live with Helen's parents anymore, so he decided to probe a little.

'Why's that?' he asked.

Emily shrugged. 'They're just the complete opposite, I guess. Too claustrophobic. Always wanting to know where I was going, telling me what I could and couldn't do. Gets a bit much after a while.'

Jack wondered if perhaps he'd gone too far the opposite way. As with all things in life, balance was the key to parenting. Not that he was the expert, of course.

'What did they make of Ethan?' he asked, knowing that his in-laws' views on Turner might give him some idea of what he was like. And, he had to be honest, he was trying to find a way to shoe-horn him into the conversation to see if Emily knew about his arrest.

Emily shrugged again. 'They didn't mind him. They didn't really meet him properly, though. Only in passing.'

Jack nodded. 'And how is he?' he asked.

'Fine. I think. Not spoken to him today.'

That answered that question, then.

'You know,' she said, 'if you really want to meet him, I could always invite him over for dinner. I could do spaghetti bolognese. I do a really good spaghetti bolognese.'

Jack's breath caught in his throat. That definitely wouldn't be a good idea. If Emily invited Ethan over for dinner, he'd definitely recognise Jack. You don't just forget the face of a police officer who nicks you for possession of drugs. In fact, he'd have to do his level best to avoid bumping into Ethan around Emily at all. 'Uh, well, I don't think you need to go to all that bother. I mean, it's a bit formal isn't it?'

'If you say so,' Emily replied. 'Maybe he could just pop over for a drink then?'

'Yeah, maybe. Probably best not to organise anything any time soon, though, what with work being like it is.'

Jack knew he was going to have to do something about this. He couldn't avoid Emily finding out about him arresting Ethan forever. But what choice did he have? He couldn't keep putting it off, nor could he ban Emily from bringing him back to the house. There was only one way that would end. He had to tread with caution as far as

Emily was concerned, but he'd also have to make sure Ethan Turner was off the scene as soon as possible.

He sat down in his armchair and felt his neck and back start to loosen, the muscles finally beginning to relax. He knew he wasn't going to get much rest over the next couple of days so he was happy to snatch an hour or two now if he could. Perhaps, if he was really lucky, he'd be able to get a bit of sleep. Oh yes. Sleep. Even the word itself felt good. As he felt his eyelids becoming heavier, he was jolted back into the real world by the ringing of his mobile phone.

'Culverhouse,' he murmured, a feeling of tired nausea starting to rise.

'Jack, it's Charles Hawes,' the Chief Constable said. 'I thought you might like to know the judge granted the forced entry warrant and we've got officers ready for you. Father Joseph Kümmel is all yours.'

41

Hilltop Farm by night looked even more bleak and depressing than Hilltop Farm by day. The team had assembled half a mile up the road, not wanting to alert the residents of Hilltop Farm to what was going on. The element of surprise was one of the biggest weapons in their arsenal. Culverhouse, leading the operation, addressed the assembled officers. He and Wendy had attended from CID, and would be directing the uniformed officers in the forced entry to Hilltop Farm.

They'd put the case to the judge that anything other than a surprise forced entry would put the retrieval of evidence at severe jeopardy. Bearing in mind the number of people living at Hilltop Farm and the allegations that had been made, the judge had agreed.

'Right. We're aiming for a quiet approach. We'll walk the last stretch to Hilltop Farm,' Culverhouse said. 'When we get there, it's hand signals only. Understood? The first line of three will cut through the gate with the oxyacety-lene torches. Then the second line of three will remove the bars and the first line will replace their torches with the bosher. We move through to the wooden gate, twat it down with the bosher and in we go. Any questions?'

'Yeah, how will we identify the building Joseph Kümmel will be in?' a young PC asked.

'You won't, because you're one of the officers staying on the front gate. But for those who'll have the luxury of meeting the delightful Father Joseph in the flesh — if he's not wearing his PJs — follow me. You all know your groups?'

The officers nodded in response.

'Right. Then let's go.'

42

Jack Culverhouse led his team of officers in silence up the dirt path towards the main body of the farm. They were less than twenty yards inside before he noticed a light come on in a brown building to their right. Culverhouse raised his hand for a moment to pause the action. After a moment, he signalled for two PCs to go towards the brown building. Culverhouse and the others carried on towards Father Joseph's living quarters.

Just as he'd turned away from the brown building and started to walk, he heard a shout from behind him.

'Stop! Police! Put the gun down!' one of the PCs yelled.

Culverhouse snapped his head towards the noise. He saw Nelson standing in the doorway of the brown building, legs apart, pointing what looked like a shotgun at the two officers.

Before he had even registered what Nelson was

holding in his hands, he was back in Suzanne Corrigan's back bedroom, face to face with the Mildenheath Ripper, watching the bright light explode from the end of the barrel. He didn't know if he'd actually seen that at the time, but he was seeing it now in glorious technicolor. He could see the edges of the blast, clear and precise, the dazzling vibrance of the gunshot searing into his retinas. The noise of the explosion came shortly after, numbing his eardrums and leaving him with a dull ringing sensation.

It was there, it was real, and he was living every single second all over again. It seemed to take forever, the seconds becoming minutes and hours. But when he slipped unnoticed back into the real world, it was as if no time had passed at all. It had been a fleeting thought, a brief electrical pulse sent through his brain, but he'd been there a lifetime.

He registered the shotgun again, sensing the panic in the minds of the two young officers, who were in line to take a cartridge should the trigger be pulled. Before he could do anything, another noise came from the direction he'd been heading in.

'Do as the man says, Nelson. It's fine,' the voice of Father Joseph Kümmel called. 'I'm willing to assist Detective Chief Inspector Culverhouse in any way I can. Although I do wish he would've knocked.'

Culverhouse's eyes never left Nelson. He held out a placating hand, as if that was going to put an end to the whole thing.

Nelson seemed to take minutes to make his decision,

although it had probably only been a second or two at most. He lowered the shotgun, pointed the barrel downward and held it slung in his right arm.

'Put it down on the floor and step away from it!' one of the young officers shouted, his voice showing far more nervousness than he would have liked.

Father Joseph nodded silently at Nelson, who complied.

'He's all yours,' Culverhouse said to the two officers, nodding towards Nelson.

'Is there any particular reason for arresting one of my most loyal parishioners, Detective Chief Inspector?' Father Joseph asked, his voice calm and composed.

'Oh, plenty, I'm sure,' Culverhouse replied. 'But for now we'll stick with pointing a gun at two police officers, shall we?' Behind him, he could hear the other officers dividing into pairs and starting to search the surrounding buildings. There would be no time to waste.

'Are you looking for something?' Father Joseph called to them, a little louder than he usually spoke.

'Don't you worry about them. We've got our own conversations to be having, you and me. At our place, if you don't mind.'

Father Joseph looked almost worried for a moment. Under his steely exterior, he seemed anxious at the prospect of leaving Hilltop Farm and heading to the police station. But, before Culverhouse could threaten him with arrest — something he'd be doing when they got in the car anyway — Father Joseph nodded and walked towards him, as both men headed for the gates.

43

Once they'd got back to the station, Father Joseph had been booked in by the custody sergeant and placed in a holding cell. Having accepted the offer of the on-call duty solicitor, the interview had been delayed to allow the solicitor to arrive, be briefed and for Culverhouse and Knight to prepare for the interview. By then, the sun was starting to rise.

With the four settled into the interview room, Culverhouse proceeded to start the recording. He gave the names of those present and stated the circumstances surrounding Father Joseph Kümmel's arrest.

'First things first, can you tell me about the community at Hilltop Farm? What's its purpose?'

Father Joseph spoke without even glancing at his solicitor. 'It's a religious community. We choose to live in segregation from the outside world in order that we are not bound by its restrictions and limitations.'

'Is that not a bit odd?' Culverhouse asked. 'I mean, you're all living in a closed community on a farm. That sounds pretty restricted and limited to me.'

'We are all restricted and limited physically, Detective Chief Inspector. Even you. We are all bound by the planet itself. What I was referring to were spiritual restrictions and limitations. They are the boundaries that we are free of, and which you on the outside world must live with every day of your lives.'

Wendy gave Culverhouse a look that reminded him he was in a recorded interview with a solicitor present.

Culverhouse decided to change the line of questioning, with a question that he hoped would catch Father Joseph off guard. 'The church at Hilltop Farm is a cult, isn't it?'

The solicitor shuffled in his chair. 'DCI Culverhouse, I don't think—'

'It's fine,' Father Joseph said, placating the solicitor with a raised palm. 'No, it is not a cult. It is a religious and spiritual community. But if your level of ignorance means that calling it a cult makes you feel better, please feel free. Cults are not illegal either.'

'No, but they're immoral, aren't they?' Wendy asked.

'And what does "immoral" mean, exactly? What is immoral to one person is completely normal to another. The human species is a varied one, as I'm sure you know only too well.'

'If you mean I never cease to be amazed at what I discover about people, you'd be right,' Wendy replied, not breaking eye contact with Father Joseph. She wanted to put him on edge, have him panicking about what she might have found out. Even though that was currently very little.

'And what have you discovered about me, exactly?' Father Joseph asked, cocking his head to the side. Wendy could sense his solicitor growing increasingly uncomfortable.

'Why? What do you think we've discovered?' Culverhouse cut in. 'What are you worried about us finding?'

Father Joseph looked at him for a few moments, then smiled and let out a small laugh. 'I don't have any concerns, Detective Chief Inspector. My main worry is that I'm having to defend the church against yet another baseless attack from the Establishment. And people wonder why we choose to segregate ourselves.'

'DCI Culverhouse, you arrested my client on suspicion of statutory rape and conspiracy to murder. As of yet you've not even had the decency to explain any of the details surrounding those allegations and have instead decided to go on this rampage of trying to besmirch his religious sensibilities. Now, could we please get to the allegations you're making?'

Culverhouse looked at the solicitor and nodded. 'Certainly. Shall we focus on the statutory rape first? We have a witness who says they saw you sexually assaulting a girl possibly aged ten or eleven. Do you have any comment?'

The solicitor interjected. 'Do you have a name for this girl, or the date on which it is alleged to have happened?'

Culverhouse looked at the solicitor and spoke with a calm voice. 'Why does that matter at this stage? So he can have a look in his diary and see if he was busy raping that day? Surely your client is able to categorically state that he's never engaged in sexual activities with a child. Why would he need names and dates?'

'Because it's usual practice, DCI Culverhouse, as well you know,' the solicitor answered. 'If my client is able to categorically prove that he was elsewhere that day or had never met the girl, the allegation collapses immediately.'

'Prove that he was elsewhere?' Culverhouse replied, laughing. 'With respect, your client lives in a closed community. Where was he meant to have gone? Popped to Sainsbury's? Gone to get his cassock dry cleaned?'

'I can only assume from your facetiousness and unwillingness to cooperate that you don't have a time, date or name of this supposed victim,' the solicitor said.

'All in good time,' Culverhouse said. 'We have our reasons for not disclosing details at this stage.'

'Yes, and I think we both know what they are,' came the brief's response.

They were interrupted by a knock on the door, which then opened, Debbie Weston's head popping round it.

'Sorry to interrupt, but can I have a word with DS Knight?' she asked.

Wendy stepped outside the room, leaving Culverhouse to explain the situation for the benefit of the recording. She could see that Debbie looked concerned. 'What's wrong?' she asked.

'We've been calling the witnesses to let them know about the arrest. We've informed them that we might have to speak to them again in more depth, depending on what comes out of the interview. All fine, but we weren't able to get hold of Sandra Kaporsky. We went round to her house, and there's no sign of her.'

'What about the officer who was meant to be watching her house?' Wendy asked.

Debbie shuffled uncomfortably. 'He reckons he didn't see anything. If you ask me, I reckon he nodded off, but that's not the official line.'

Wendy sighed. If that was true, it was incompetence of the highest order. But at the same time she knew what long, exhausting shifts could do to an officer. 'Maybe she's gone out or away for a couple of days,' Wendy said. 'It happens.'

'Normally I'd agree with you, but this is different. Her next-door neighbour said Sandra left the house in her car at one-thirty this morning — something she never does. Not only that, but when we rang her mobile, we could hear it ringing inside the house. She's gone out in the dead of night, left her phone at home and hasn't returned by the morning. Bit weird, wouldn't you say?'

Wendy had to admit that it was.

44

The initial interview with Father Joseph had uncovered next to nothing. He'd denied knowing the names of any of the people who'd disappeared from the farm. He claimed that he wasn't on first-name terms with most of the people in the community, preferring instead to be a more distant leader.

Their only real hope now seemed to rest on uncovering some sort of evidence at Hilltop Farm which they could use to pin down the crimes that had been committed. So far, there was no news from the search teams. They had recovered some documentation, but none of it seemed relevant or useful in any way. They needed something big. If someone had been committing murders at the farm and there were no vehicles going in or out at any point, logic dictated that the bodies must still be on the farm somewhere. But that would take time, and time was running out.

Ordinarily, they could only hold someone in custody for twenty-four hours before they must either arrest or charge them. Within that time, the police would have to build a strong enough case for the Crown Prosecution Service to be happy enough that there was a good chance of a conviction. Without that, they'd recommend the detainee was released. Trials were expensive, and the CPS weren't keen on taking on any they weren't almost certain they could win.

Arrests for murder, though, could be granted an extension of a further twelve hours. But that was only when authorised by an officer ranking Superintendent or above. Culverhouse had left it to Wendy to request the extension. Far from wanting to have to grovel to someone at Milton House, she'd gone straight to Chief Constable Charles Hawes.

Hawes's office smelt of coffee, and Wendy didn't suppose the windows had been opened in months.

'Sir, we'd like to get your authorisation on an extension of custody for Father Joseph Kümmel. He's proving to be a difficult suspect. Our search teams are going to need more time to conduct an effective search of Hilltop Farm,' she said, having rehearsed the wording on her way up there.

'In principle that's fine,' the Chief Constable said, 'but we need to weigh up the advantages and disadvantages. If we've given a custody extension and still find nothing, then want to come back at a later date and arrest and charge him, it's not going to look good.'

'I understand that, sir, but without the extension

there's going to be no way in hell of being able to gather the evidence we need to charge him. We're potentially looking at ground-penetrating radar and excavations. It's not the sort of thing that we can turn around inside a few hours.'

Hawes leaned back in his chair. 'That's big. Are you confident that with the extra time you'll be able to find something substantial? Enough that we'll be able to charge and won't end up with a load of egg on our faces?'

Wendy paused for a moment, swallowed hard and then answered. 'Yes, sir,' she lied. 'I'm confident.'

Hawes looked at her for a second or two. 'Right. Well, on your head be it.'

45

With the custody extension granted, Culverhouse at least felt that he had a little more breathing space. They had enough to do in the meantime, and time was ticking away. Searches at Hilltop Farm were ongoing, as were interviews with Father Joseph. Everything was being cross-checked and verified with the witnesses to try and pin down some more definite information. With luck, they'd find something that could result in the CPS recommending they charge him.

The obvious thought had gone through his mind. Had they decided to arrest him too soon? Had they shot themselves in the foot by jumping in too early? He didn't think so. He hoped not. Had they waited, Father Joseph would've had all sorts of opportunities to hide evidence or carry on with his crimes. When a serious crime was reported, it was his duty to ensure it was investigated quickly, efficiently, and the suspected party brought in for questioning. The easiest way to do that was through an arrest.

Under the Police and Criminal Evidence Act, an arrest gave them the right to detain the suspect for up to twenty-four hours — thirty-six in serious cases such as murder — and even that could be extended to ninety-six hours with the permission of a court judge. Being arrested in itself wasn't any indicator of guilt, and the police were technically at liberty to arrest anyone for anything. Its main purpose was to lock in that twenty-four hour period and allow them to conduct a more thorough search of premises.

With their extension, they had until tomorrow morning to either charge or release Father Joseph Kümmel. Culverhouse knew which he would prefer. Although he'd not been convinced of any wrongdoing at Hilltop Farm initially, the witness statements he'd seen were conclusive in his eyes. Anything that mentioned a young girl, barely three years younger than his own daughter, being sexually assaulted was sure to ignite the fire in his belly.

There was still no news on Sandra Kaporsky, either. Culverhouse had decided they'd give it another couple of hours, then they'd put a marker out on her vehicle. They were more worried for her own safety than anything else. In the meantime, he had other business to attend to.

He shrugged on his jacket, grabbed his car keys and headed for the car park. As he walked to his car, he fingered the small torn-out piece of paper in his jacket pocket. Good. It was still there.

He turned left out of the car park and up in the direction of Allerdale Road. When he got there, he parked his car up outside a house and walked the final couple of dozen yards to the phone box, knowing he would've stayed clear of any CCTV cameras. This was the phone box they'd received the initial anonymous phone call from. He knew from his own experience and frustrations how much of a black spot it was in terms of traceability.

He pulled open the door and stepped inside. Taking a handkerchief from his pocket, he picked up the receiver with the handkerchief and held it next to his ear. With another hankie, he took the pound coin from his pocket, rubbing it with the cotton to ensure his prints weren't anywhere on the coin, and pushed it into the coin slot. It was probably overkill, but he couldn't afford to be too careful in his position. Then he took the torn out piece of paper from his jacket pocket and dialled the number written on it, pushing the numbers on the keypad with his knuckle.

After a few moments, the phone started to ring, followed by the recognisable click of the call connecting.

'Yeah?' came the response at the other end.

'Ethan?' Jack asked, disguising his voice.

'Who's asking?'

'Friend of a friend. Listen, I need sorting out. I'm told you're the man.'

'You were told wrong,' Ethan replied. 'Laters.'

'Wait,' Jack replied. 'I'm serious. I'm desperate. I'm in some real fucking shit here and I gotta get it sorted.'

There were a few seconds of silence before Ethan spoke. 'Who's your mate?'

Jack thought on his feet and reacted quickly. 'What, you think I'm fucking stupid? You think I'm gonna name names?'

'Alright, alright,' Ethan replied. 'What you looking for?'

Jack felt a sense of relief. 'Base.'

'Alright. How much we talking?'

He did a quick bit of mental arithmetic. Amphetamine was a class-A drug. Fifty grams should do it.

'Fifty,' he replied.

'Fifty mil?'

Culverhouse put on the angry act again. 'Fuck off, man. You think I'm gonna be shittin' my Calvins over fifty mil? I'm talkin' grams, boss.'

'Fifty G? Shit. You know that ain't gonna be cheap.'

'I know. How much?'

Ethan seemed to be thinking for a second. 'Call it two large.'

Culverhouse's eyes almost popped out on stalks. He knew fifty grams of amphetamine would probably only be worth five to eight hundred pounds, depending on the quality. Around Mildenheath, probably nearer five hundred. 'You havin' a fuckin' laugh?' he replied, still in character.

'Thought you were desperate,' Ethan replied. 'You know what strings I gotta pull to get that sort of quantity any time soon? Next time, get your fuckin' shit together sooner. Take it or leave it.'

Culverhouse took a step back for a moment. This was the scum his daughter was hanging around with. And at the end of the day, it didn't matter one jot what money Ethan wanted for the drugs. He wasn't going to be getting a penny either way. Having him banged up in a prison cell and five hundred quid in debt to drug dealers was going to be sweet music to Jack's ears.

'Two large. But I want it tonight,' he said. 'No fuckin' about, either. Albert Road car park, back of the chippy. Eight-thirty.'

'Alright. What number can I get you on?'

'You can't,' Culverhouse replied. 'You're there or you're fuckin' mince.'

He put the phone down, waited for a couple of seconds to compose himself, then left the phone box, making sure to wipe the handle with his handkerchief on the way out.

He drove back into town and parked up in the church car park. He locked his car, walked in through the large stone archway and headed towards the war memorial.

There were a number of benches scattered around, the church's grounds seeming like the perfect place to go for a nice afternoon walk — until you noticed the winos and alcoholics cluttering up the benches. He clocked one man sitting with a can of cider. He couldn't recall his name, but he knew he had form. He walked over and sat next to him.

'Nice day,' he said, eventually.

'I wouldn't know, *officer*,' the man said, almost spitting the last word, the reek of sweet alcohol assaulting Jack's nostrils.

'Could be even better, mind. Fancy earning fifty quid?' He could almost sense the man's ears pricking up.

'Depends. I ain't gonna suck you off if that's what you're after.'

Culverhouse allowed himself to smirk. 'Not half as attractive an offer as that, I'm afraid. I need you to make a phone call. That's all.'

'Fifty quid for a phone call?' the man asked, his eyes narrowing. 'Who to?'

'101. Police non-emergency number. I want you to tell them there's a big drugs deal going down in the Albert Road car park at half-eight tonight. Behind the chip shop.'

'That's it?'

'That's it.'

'Right. Yeah, I'll just get my fuckin' iPhone out then, shall I?' the man said. 'Pound for a phone box?'

'You'll get nothing til it's done,' Culverhouse replied. 'If you've got no money, go to the police station and tell them there. Tell them you overheard it being arranged and one of the blokes threatened you. Skinny kid, mousy hair. He threatened you to keep quiet, but you aren't having it.'

'You think they're gonna swallow that?' the man said, laughing.

'That's your problem, not mine,' Culverhouse replied. 'Just you make sure uniform are there at half eight tonight.

That's all you've got to do. How you manage that is up to you.'

'And why can't you do it? You're the copper.'

'Procedural and operational difficulties,' Culverhouse said, standing up. 'Just you make sure it's done and you'll have the money. Same time tomorrow, same place.'

'What's this? Some sort of sting? Trying to entrap me?'

'Oh yeah. Totally. Going to get you done for making a phone call with intent. Over-eagerness to report a crime. Now tell me. Where, when, who?'

The man sighed. 'Albert Road car park, behind the chip shop, half eight. Some skinny shit with mousey hair.'

Culverhouse nodded and started to walk back to his car.

'Hundred quid,' the man called out after him.

Culverhouse raised a thumb in the air without looking behind him, and carried on towards the car park.

46

Wendy was about to head into the interview room to speak to Father Joseph with DCI Culverhouse again when Steve Wing stopped her.

'I've just had a call which might interest you,' he said, between mouthfuls of sausage roll.

'Can it wait, Steve?' Wendy said, keen not to waste any more time.

'Uh, not if you're going to the interview room, no. This is probably something you'll want to know about first.'

Although Steve had a reputation for pratting about at times, Wendy could see by the look on his face that the message was something worth hearing.

'Go on.'

'Earlier today I spoke to James Aston again, formerly called Harry Gallagher. He seemed a bit uneasy but I just put that down to the situation, you know. Father Joseph being in custody, all the memories coming flooding back and that. I didn't think much of it at the time, but the thing is he just called me back. He said he didn't want to sound as if he was panicking, but he hasn't had any messages from Ben since yesterday.'

'So what? I thought he was sending the camera drone over weekly?' Wendy said.

'He was. But recently he's been doing it every day. He said he was worried because Ben always leaves a message, without fail. Even if it's just to say "no news", he always does it. James said he sort of treated it like a dead man's switch: if Ben didn't leave a message, he'd assume it was because he was unable to.'

Wendy shuffled uncomfortably. 'He might be ill or something.'

'Might be,' Steve said. 'But James seemed pretty convinced something was wrong.'

She thought about this for a moment. 'I think we have to bear in mind that things have changed pretty quickly. Father Joseph's in custody, there are officers searching the farm for evidence. I should imagine he either thinks there's no use sending messages out or it's passed him by because of everything that's going on.'

Steve put on an uneasy smile, and shook his head. 'I dunno. The search officers are making a point of keeping things respectful where they can. They've not just gone in and turned the place upside down. The church organisers and rankers are under twenty-four hour watch. The residents themselves aren't being harassed or anything. Other than being asked if they want to provide witness statements, that is.'

'And are they?' Wendy asked.

'Not really. Most are supportive of the church and are pissed off that we're trying to ruin things for them. The atmosphere's pretty hostile for a religious community. Kind of a good thing, I guess, as anyone who *does* want to talk, will. At least we're not wasting our time speaking to people who'll try to deflect from the issues when we could be using those officers to search. We're short-staffed enough as it is over there. The place is huge.'

Wendy considered her options. 'Right. I'd say the best way forward is to try and locate Ben Gallagher at the farm. People will know where he is, or where he's meant to be. Speak to James Aston again and get him to mark on an aerial map where Ben's lodging is. We'll make sure officers keep a specific eye out for him. Is there any chance he could've escaped?'

Steve shook his head. 'No. Only way out is through the main gate, as we know, and there are officers stationed on it. He's definitely still in there somewhere. The only question is whether he's alive or dead.'

47

The conversation with Steve Wing played on Wendy's mind through the whole of the second interview with Father Joseph Kümmel. There had now been a number of allegations of people going missing from Hilltop Farm over the years, and apart from the ones who escaped and had come forward, there were still gaps. Either those people had also managed to escape — although how, Wendy didn't know, seeing as the only people able to escape were those with access to the outside world anyway — or they never left the farm at all.

The sense of what that meant wasn't lost on Wendy. If Ben Gallagher had been identified as the source of the information leak, there was every chance he would have been punished for it. And that meant there'd likely have been another murder at Hilltop Farm. This time, though, it would have been one that they could have avoided.

The potential ramifications of that were huge. They

just didn't bear thinking about. The media coverage would be never ending. It would almost certainly mean the end of Mildenheath CID as a self-sufficient satellite unit. And it would put another nail in the coffin for Jack Culverhouse's career. After all, there were only so many second chances a man could have. Sooner or later, the hammer had to fall.

For now, Wendy had to pray that Ben Gallagher was found alive and well. She knew, though, that was unlikely.

She blinked a couple of times, desperate to stop her mind from wandering and to focus on the task in hand. She realised she'd completely zoned out and had lost the thread of the interview.

'The fact of the matter is, these are serious allegations and you've not, as of yet, provided a single shred of evidence to back these up,' Father Joseph's solicitor said. 'You and I are both well aware of the sort of manner in which people tend to view closed religious communities. There's a certain stigma attached. And yes, some people have either left of their own accord or been asked to leave. If their families choose not to join them, it's only natural that those people would feel a resentment against the church. But it is not right that vicious allegations made by those people should result in the sort of baseless action we've seen the police taking recently.'

Culverhouse was leaning back in his chair, arms folded. 'Very good, Mr Winder. Extraordinarily well rehearsed. Almost textbook.'

'If you've not got anything constructive to add, Detective Chief Inspector, then perhaps we should—'

'Oh, I've got plenty to add,' Culverhouse said, leaning forward, elbows on desk. 'Perhaps we could begin with some specifics. What does the name Amy Kemp mean to you?'

Wendy looked at Father Joseph, trying to detect the telltale flickers of recognition on his face. There were none. He was either completely unaware of who Amy Kemp was, or he was an expert liar.

'Not a whole lot, I'm afraid,' Father Joseph replied. 'Should it?'

'She was a member of your church,' Culverhouse said. 'Until recently, that is. She's not been seen in the past couple of days. Not since one of the residents at Hilltop Farm saw her being apprehended while trying to make a run for it.'

Wendy thought she could see Father Joseph's jaw clench slightly. She didn't want to tell him she'd got the information from Ben Gallagher via his brother. For now, she was keeping her cards close to her chest.

'They must be mistaken. I'm not aware of her at all.'

The solicitor interjected. 'Detective Chief Inspector, do you have any official record showing that this Amy Kemp ever actually lived at Hilltop Farm?'

Wendy looked at Jack. They both knew there were no official records of any of the residents at Hilltop Farm.

'I'm more interested at the moment in what your client has to say about her disappearance,' Culverhouse replied.

'You and I both know that someone can only disappear if they existed in the first place. So, you need to provide us with some evidence that she ever actually existed if you want us to be able to help you find out if she's disappeared. Now, is there any evidence of her existence at the farm or can we just put this down as being another malicious rumour?'

Culverhouse was silent, calm, for a moment before speaking. 'All I would advise your client to be aware of is that it's only a matter of time before the paper trail leads us precisely there. It would be wise for him to speak now if he thinks there's even the slightest chance we might have hit the nail on the head here.'

Father Joseph remained silent.

It was Wendy's turn to speak. 'What about Ben Gallagher?' she said, having spoken barely a word since entering the interview room. This time, she could swear she saw Father Joseph's face twitch, almost imperceptibly, but it was definitely there if you were looking for it.

'I'm afraid you're going to need to provide more than that, Detective Sergeant,' the solicitor replied.

'Perhaps it would be good for your client to speak for himself,' Wendy offered. 'After all, he's the one under arrest. He's the one who needs to prove his innocence.'

'On the contrary,' the solicitor said, leaning forward with a cocky smile. 'Under English law, the onus is on you to prove guilt. Not for my client to prove innocence.'

Wendy looked Father Joseph in the eye. She took a gamble on the presumption that she had nothing to lose. If she gave Father Joseph this information, what could he do with it from a prison cell? Nothing. It would mean they'd have to make absolutely certain they got permission to charge him from the CPS, though. If Father Joseph got back to Hilltop Farm with this information under his belt, it could spell curtains for the whole investigation. But the information itself would greatly increase their chances of being able to charge him. She took the plunge.

'See, we can prove that Ben Gallagher was or is a resident of Hilltop Farm,' Wendy said. 'His brother, Harry, left Hilltop Farm some time ago, didn't he? That name must certainly ring a bell for you, too. He was one of your recruiters. Do you remember him?'

'No comment,' Father Joseph replied.

Wendy smiled inwardly. It was the first time he'd no commented and she knew that could only mean one thing. It was time to drive the stake home.

'I presume you weren't aware that Harry Gallagher has been flying a camera drone over Hilltop Farm on a weekly basis?' Wendy asked, watching closely as Father Joseph's eyes flickered slightly, his jaw tightening as she spoke. 'No, neither were we until recently. It seems that Ben Gallagher, his brother, had been leaving messages for the camera drone. He was passing information out of the farm. But then again you knew this, didn't you? And that's why Ben Gallagher hasn't been seen or heard from since yesterday either, isn't it?'

As she finished speaking, she could see by the look on Father Joseph's face that it certainly wasn't the reason why Ben Gallagher hadn't been seen or heard from. She could see that this was almost certainly the first he'd heard of

Harry Gallagher's camera drone. His face was pure restrained fury, the look of a man who'd just found out he'd been betrayed. Wendy knew in that moment that there was more behind Ben Gallagher's lack of contact with his brother since yesterday.

'Why would someone who lives at Hilltop Farm and plays an active part in the church community want to pass information to the outside?' Culverhouse asked Father Joseph. 'I mean, you can hardly say it's a malicious attempt to attack the church, can you?'

Father Joseph remained silent.

'Detectives, are you going to enlighten us as to what this supposed information was?' the solicitor asked. 'Because you don't need me to remind you that time is running out and you've yet to offer any evidence at all of any crimes having been committed other than hearsay and a couple of people who haven't been heard from in a day or two.'

For just a moment, Wendy could swear she saw the faintest flicker of a smile cross Father Joseph's face. Just as she was trying to interpret what it might have meant, there was a knock at the door. Wendy announced her departure for the benefit of the tape and left the room.

Outside, she was met by a beaming Frank Vine.

'Got some intel from Hilltop Farm that might interest you,' he said, clutching a notepad. 'Get this. They've found cyanide.'

Wendy's eyebrows shot up. 'Cyanide?'

'Yep. Loads of it. About two kilos of the stuff. Enough to kill four thousand people.'

'Jesus fucking Christ.'

'Indeed. Makes you wonder about ol' JC if that's what he's got his followers doing, eh? All the info's here,' he said, passing over the notepad. 'Thought you might like to drop that one on him. It's being taken in for further analysis, but the boys were pretty certain.'

Wendy looked down at the notepad, allowed herself to smile for a moment, then re-entered the interview room.

48

'Sorry about that,' Wendy said as she sat back down, 'but I'm afraid it does have a bearing on things going on in this room.' She looked at Culverhouse, who had clearly spotted that something big was going on.

'Well it'd better be good, Detective Sergeant, because my client has been extremely helpful to you so far — considering the circumstances. And by my watch it's approaching mealtime. I'm sure you don't need me to remind you of your responsibilities with regards to his welfare.'

'Not at all,' Wendy said with a wry smile. 'He can have my lunch, if he likes. I didn't get a chance to have any of it. It's a rare occasion that I get to eat at mealtimes, if at all, but we'll do all we can to ensure your client's needs are met. Now, if I may just alter the track of the conversation slightly, my colleague just informed me that the search of Hilltop Farm has found something rather intriguing.' She left that hanging in the air for a few seconds. 'Cyanide. Two kilos of it. Do you have any comment?'

Father Joseph's solicitor leaned forward and opened his mouth to speak before Father Joseph raised his hand to silence him.

'Is it illegal to possess cyanide in this country, Detective Sergeant?' he asked, his solicitor sitting meekly by his side.

Wendy suspected this might be his plan of attack. 'Not at this present time, no.'

'Then I fail to see what relevance it has to your investigation,' came the curt response.

'The relevance,' Wendy replied, leaning forward, 'is that we're investigating potential murders at Hilltop Farm. The same Hilltop Farm where we have just discovered a large quantity of cyanide, a compound which can kill people in extremely small doses. That is the relevance.'

The solicitor piped up again. 'With respect, Detective Sergeant Knight, that is circumstantial at best and you know it. Cyanide has many legitimate uses beyond the realms of second-rate crime fiction. And you don't need me to remind you that, even on the extremely unlikely off-chance that you were to find victims of cyanide poisoning, the cyanide itself would still be purely circumstantial. You still have nothing to tie my client to any crime whatsoever.'

Wendy decided to throw Father Joseph a curveball. She ignored the solicitor and went straight for the jugular.

'Father Joseph, perhaps you could enlighten us by

letting us know what legal and legitimate uses you have for cyanide at Hilltop Farm.'

He leaned forward, resting his forearms on the table, a small smile appearing across his face. 'Pest control. Medical uses. Sculpture.'

'Sculpture?' Wendy asked.

'It's often used to give a dark blue tint to cast bronze when painted on. It's a quite striking and desirable look.'

'Funny. We don't recall seeing many bronze statues at Hilltop Farm. Do you remember seeing any, sir?' Wendy asked Culverhouse.

'Can't say I do.'

'That is because we haven't started yet. We are planning for our future,' Father Joseph said. 'I feel it's always important to plan ahead.'

'I see,' Wendy said, smiling to humour him. 'And what medical uses do you have for cyanide?'

'We use it for testing ketone body levels in the urine of diabetic parishioners,' he replied, with a tone that made it sound as though it was a question he was asked all the time.

'Have many diabetics coming to you for help, do you?' Culverhouse chimed in.

'We have a small handful in the church. Nowhere near the percentage you'd see in the outside world, though. We tend not to force sugars and fats on our children. We promote a balanced, healthy, natural diet. But yes, of course there are a small number of people with diabetes.'

'Do you not think they'd be better off being treated in a hospital, by doctors?' Wendy asked.

'I don't think you quite grasp the idea of a closed community, Detective Sergeant. We have our own doctors. They are perfectly capable of treating most illnesses.'

Somehow, Wendy doubted this. She wondered how many people had died over the years through medical neglect.

'Detective Sergeant Knight, are you going to charge my client or are you going to finally admit that you have not one shred of evidence to hold against him?' the solicitor asked.

Wendy wished she could answer that question.

49

By nine-thirty, Culverhouse was starting to worry. He'd spent enough time in and around the custody suite over the past few hours to have known if Ethan Turner had been booked in. There were free cells, and Mildenheath was by far the closest station, so he'd definitely be brought here. But an hour after the time the deal had been arranged for, there was still no sign of him having been arrested. That meant he could only assume one thing: it hadn't happened.

He knew he was skating on thin ice, trying to manage all this at the same time as his team were trying to pin evidence on Father Joseph Kümmel and Hilltop Farm, but he had no choice. He'd found out what Ethan Turner was all about and there was no way he was going to allow his daughter to get involved with pondlife like that. How would he ever forgive himself if he came home and found her gone, lying dead on a park bench somewhere, having been injected with some street shit? He couldn't. And, not for the first time, the constraints of the law had failed him and he was going to have to take measures into his own hands.

Back at the Allerdale Road phone box, he called Ethan again, taking the same precautions as last time in terms of fingerprints.

'Yeah?' Ethan said, answering the phone.

'What the fuck was that all about?' Culverhouse asked, in his disguised voice.

'Dunno what you mean. Who's this?'

'Where the fuck were you?' Culverhouse asked, immediately regretting it. What if Ethan or one of his contacts had been there, and had seen the police presence? Culverhouse would've just given himself away immediately, proving he hadn't been there.

'Nowhere. I got delayed. It ain't fuckin' easy to get hold of fifty G that quick, you know?'

It seemed plausible. He might have a second chance. 'Right. How long?'

'Like ten minutes. Literally. My boy's coming over with it now. I woulda rung to let you know, but you didn't leave no number.'

'Half an hour. Ten o'clock, behind the shops on Allerdale Road in Mildenheath. Got it?'

'Fuck's sake, man. That's gonna be tight on time.'

'Your problem. Not mine. Get your *boy* to hurry the fuck up.'

Culverhouse put the phone down, wiped his prints

from the door handle and walked the short distance to the parade of shops near the phone box. Down the side of the parade was an access staircase for the flats above. The concrete faced the back of the shops, allowing him to see anyone walking from the road to behind the parade, whilst remaining in the shadows himself. He sat down four or five steps up — just enough to be out of sight but able to reach the ground quickly enough — and waited.

Ethan was, surprisingly, on time. Culverhouse dreaded to think of the speeds he must've been doing to have got here that quickly, but he didn't really care right now. He had only one thing on his mind.

He watched as Ethan walked past the bottom of the staircase, hands shoved into his jacket pockets, before disappearing behind the side wall and behind the shops. Jack stood, tiptoed down the steps, and picked up a snapped wooden broom handle he'd found amongst the general detritus behind the shops earlier. He stepped up behind Ethan, before wrapping the broom handle in front of his neck and pulling it back with his free hand.

Ethan was now pressed up against him, wriggling his legs. Jack lifted the broom handle higher, taking Ethan off his feet as he struggled with his hands to release the pressure on his throat.

Jack walked him the few feet to his right and pressed him against the wall, releasing the broken broom handle. He pushed his forearm into the back of Ethan's head, watching his face contort as it scraped against the brick wall.

'Now, you're going to listen to me and you're going to listen to me good,' Jack said, feeling the adrenaline coursing through his body. 'Fifty grams of amphet is enough to send you down for a good few months, if not more. I know what you and your friends are up to. And you know what? Frankly I don't give a shit. I spend my days locking up bigger people than you. Now, tell me. Does Emily know what you're like?'

'Emily who?' Ethan said, his voice muffled as he tried to speak.

'Don't fucking give me that,' Culverhouse said, pushing Ethan's face even harder into the wall, adding a bit of lateral force to make sure he lost another layer of skin. 'I know who you are. I know your number. I know where you live. And I know what you do. I know what you are. And if you want your contacts knowing that you hang around with young girls, that's fine with me. I can let them know that. And when you're sick and tired of having your tyres let down and your house firebombed, I can give you a helping hand by having you banged up for dealing. That'll be nice, won't it? You'll have a break for a few months, or maybe a year or two. At least inside you won't have to worry about the firebombings. It'll be razor blades in your porridge and big black cocks up your arse instead. That sound like a step up, does it? Because on the other hand you could just cut off all contact with Emily and it'll all go away until the next time you try speaking to her. Do I make myself understood?'

Ethan seemed to be trying to nod. 'Yeah. Yeah I got it.'

Culverhouse could sense that he meant it. He'd learnt to identify the smell of pure fear as easily as he could smell the piss running down the inside of Ethan Turner's leg.

'Good. Now I'm going to let go of you and you're going to stay exactly where you are. You're going to count to a hundred, then you're going to go home, stick *Question Time* on and enjoy a nice cup of Horlicks. Alright?'

'Yeah,' Ethan squeaked.

Culverhouse gave his face one last shove into the wall, then turned and made his way back towards his car.

50

Wendy had been almost completely unable to get any sleep that night. She hadn't gone home, and had instead opted to bed down in the office with a sleeping bag. It wasn't technically the done thing any more, with overtime pay being cut and occupational health practices being more forced on officers than encouraged. But going home and coming back would be completely futile. Not only would she waste time making the journey each way, but the likelihood was that she'd be woken by a phone call almost immediately and have to come back anyway. At least this way she was already here.

There was, by now, almost nothing she could do. They'd drawn a blank in terms of being able to pin the information they had on Father Joseph, and they were now completely reliant on some physical evidence turning up at Hilltop Farm. But time was very quickly ticking away.

She'd tried to force herself to sleep, knowing fate was

now largely out of her hands. She knew her phone would ring as soon as anything was found, but the more she willed herself to sleep the more frustrated she got, and the harder she found it to relax. She wondered if she'd be better off just getting up and doing something. She knew she wouldn't be functioning as well as she would be after sleep, though. After a while, she'd managed to nod off and had woken up with a stiff neck and a throat that felt like she'd swallowed razors.

Shortly before midday, Culverhouse returned from Hilltop Farm, where he'd gone earlier that morning to go through any potential evidence that had been found. Officers with ground-penetrating radar had been out first thing, but had found nothing of interest. If there were any dead bodies at Hilltop Farm, they certainly weren't buried in the fields.

Documentation had been severely limited, too. Jack knew that even the most reclusive and closed community would still have some sort of paperwork, even if it was something internal. He suspected that it had all been burnt long ago, or perhaps that nothing was kept. No paper trail, no evidence. The whole case was now starting to look worryingly thin.

Wendy was also worried about what she'd revealed to Father Joseph about Ben Gallagher. If Ben was actually alive and well on the farm, what would Father Joseph do to him if they had to release him? She didn't know if she could live with that guilt. She had to hope they'd find something before the custody deadline.

'Anything?' she asked Culverhouse when he returned, although she could see from the look of thunder on his face that the answer would be negative.

'No. Nothing.'

'What about Ben Gallagher?' she asked.

'No sign of him,' Culverhouse replied quietly, almost whispering.

'Do you think he could've escaped somehow?'

'Don't see how. The only way out is the main gate, and that's manned by us.'

Wendy couldn't see how this could be possible. 'But people can't just go missing like that. They can't disappear into thin air. He's got to be on that farm somewhere and there've got to be others.'

'We've searched the whole fucking place, Knight. They've had GPR scanning the fields to see if anything was buried there, the buildings have been checked. There's nothing.'

'What about incineration? What if they've been burnt, or put in an acid bath or something?'

Culverhouse shook his head. 'Burning would still leave something. Human bodies don't burn brilliantly. And if they'd used chemicals there'd be some sort of sign of it. There's nothing. No drums, nothing like that. And before you ask, no, I don't think they've been fed to the bloody pigs. Even they'd leave a trace of some sort. Problem is, we're very fucking short on time now.'

'What about an extension?' Wendy asked. A judge

would be able to grant a custody extension to ninety-six hours. She knew it could well be their only hope.

'It's crossed my mind. It's all we've got. I was hoping we'd have something more concrete by now, though.'

Wendy looked at her watch. 'We haven't got long. If we're going to apply for an extension we'll need to inform the custody sergeant.'

Culverhouse nodded as he fished into his trouser pocket to pull out his ringing mobile phone. 'I'll get onto it,' he said before answering. 'Culverhouse.' His face looked stoic as he listened to the voice on the other end of the phone. 'Right. I see. Thanks. And have there been any other sightings since? Right. Thanks.' He pursed his lips as he locked his phone and put it back in his pocket.

'Trouble?' Wendy asked.

'Could be. Sandra Kaporsky's car was spotted by ANPR cameras on the A354, heading towards the south coast. It was last spotted just after Blandford Forum, and hasn't been picked up since. They're going to send some local officers down to keep an eye out.'

'Lulworth Cove,' Wendy said. 'Sandra said she often visited the area. She's got friends there. That's where she'll be.'

'Strange time for a fucking holiday,' Culverhouse replied.

Even stranger that she chose to leave in the dead of night and not take her mobile phone, Wendy thought.

51

There were some aspects of policing that were truly horrendous. Many people assumed these to be things like seeing dead bodies and coming face to face with murderers. True, they weren't nice parts of the job, but the truth was you became somewhat desensitised to them.

Then there were other things which never grew old. The thrill of the chase, the excitement when an arrest was finally carried out. But one of the most nerve-wracking experiences for Wendy was waiting for the CPS's recommendation to charge or release. It was on a par with waiting to find out whether the magistrate had given them permission for a custody extension.

It wasn't something Jack relished either. But he had the added advantage of being Mildenheath Police's representative at the hearing, which was, as per usual, short and informal. The magistrate would only be able to grant a detention extension for a further 36 hours at a time, with a maximum of 96 hours in total. But Jack knew that any extension at all was far from guaranteed.

'First of all, can you explain the circumstances as to why you believe the detainee should remain in police custody, as opposed to being released on bail?' the magistrate asked.

Culverhouse straightened his tie and gave his well-rehearsed response. 'We believe the detainee poses a considerable threat to the residents at Hilltop Farm. Furthermore, we believe that releasing him will give him the opportunity to destroy or otherwise tamper with potential evidence.'

The magistrate nodded and looked down at the papers in front of her. 'And what evidence do you believe is in existence, which could potentially be destroyed or tampered with?'

'We're unsure at this stage, ma'am,' Culverhouse replied. 'It seems that record-keeping at the address has been scant, to say the least.'

'I understand you have a dozen officers at the scene, and that they've been there for almost thirty-six hours,' the magistrate said.

'That's correct, ma'am.'

'Yet you have uncovered no evidence, and there are areas of the farm that you still need to search?'

'In part, ma'am. We found a large quantity of cyanide at the farm, which in itself isn't illegal but could be an indicator of nefarious use.'

'But it could also be an indicator of legitimate, legal and responsible use?'

Culverhouse shuffled in his seat. 'That's correct, ma'am.'

'And is there anything that could even be considered circumstantial, evidentially, that points to the detainee having committed a crime that would warrant an extended detention?'

'We have some witness reports, ma'am.'

'Ah yes. Witness reports,' she said, rifling through the papers in front of her. 'I had a brief look at those. No dates, no times, no names of victims. A distinct lack of detail, in fact. Is that detail that you're going to be able to flesh out inside the next thirty-six hours?'

'We hope so, ma'am,' Culverhouse replied.

'You hope so?' The grey-haired magistrate raised her eyebrows and peered at Culverhouse across the table, over the top of her glasses. 'Detective Chief Inspector, as you well know, the extension of detention is a serious matter and a decision which must not be taken lightly. The option is not there to be taken on a whim, lest every officer leading a case applies for it and makes the whole twenty-four hour limit futile. It'd make a mockery of the system.'

'I understand that, ma'am, but in this particular case we really do need more time. Questioning of the suspect hasn't yet proved successful. But in recent interviews we've seen a considerable improvement in—'

'Detective Chief Inspector, I am not interested in considerable improvements. I'm interested in lawful detention. You have not provided me with any indication that the detainee constitutes a threat to himself, to anyone else or to the preservation of evidence. Your witnesses — as useful as they may or may not have been — have not been named, could not possibly be identified due to the paucity of information they've provided and in any case do not live in the vicinity of Hilltop Farm. I'm afraid I fail to see any plausible reason for extending the detention limit in this case.'

Culverhouse felt his jaw tighten and the anger rise up inside him, but he knew this was not the place for him to channel it. He couldn't overturn a magistrate's decision. The decision had been made. Father Joseph Kümmel would have to be released.

52

PC Karim Rashid was starting to get pretty sick of being given the shitty jobs. By now, he was starting to wonder whether policing on the whole was just one great big shitty job.

He'd expected to be out on the streets, responding to 999 calls and arresting criminals. Instead, he spent most of his time escorting alcoholics from off-licences they'd been banned from and finding old women lying dead in puddles of piss in their nicotine-stained flats. He'd had a short frisson of excitement during the Ripper case a while back, and had been one of the officers out on the streets on the night of one of the murders. He'd hoped he'd be the one to finally find and arrest the Ripper, but instead he'd been the one who'd discovered the victim dead in a car park.

Story of his life.

He'd moved south to Mildenheath from Leicester after finishing university. His three older brothers had all turned to a life of crime early on, and he'd been determined not to go the same way. They'd all struggled at school, but he tended to find academia much easier. That gave him something to work towards. Over time, he'd managed to cut almost all ties with his old life back home. Now he'd started to put some of his family's wrongs right, by working on the other side of the fence. It felt weird calling Leicester home. Mildenheath was home now. But he was now starting to doubt whether a career in the police was for him.

It all looked great at first. Even when he'd been asked to join a team combing Hilltop Farm for evidence of a murder cult, he'd been excited. How could you not be when it was put to you like that? But, of course, it wasn't all fun and games. In fact it wasn't fun at all. Instead, he was on his hands and knees in the dirt and dust rifling through cupboards and dirty old barns trying to find something they didn't even know existed.

Evidence of murder was what they'd been told to look for. Usually, that meant a dead body. The brief was that had murders been committed, it was likely the bodies were on the farm. But so far they'd found no trace of that at all. All he'd had were bizarre encounters with the people who lived here, who'd been quite happy to go out of their way to make life difficult for them. They wouldn't answer any questions and seemed to be more offended and upset at the police intrusion. No helping some people, he thought to himself. None of them seemed happy to be here. Not *truly* happy, anyway. Accepting of their situation, yes. Deeply, spiritually happy? No. He'd seen that look in people's eyes too many times when he was younger to know that it wasn't true happiness.

And here he was, on his hands and knees, scrabbling about in a glorified old shed, searching for something, although he didn't know what. The irony wasn't lost on Karim.

What did they expect him to find, exactly? The only dead bodies he'd come across here were rats. Calling the building a 'medical centre' was an absolute joke. He knew he wouldn't want to be treated in here. It looked like something out of the historical medical rooms in the London Dungeon. He wouldn't be surprised to find leeches and medieval implements. But the truth was that there was very little in here at all.

He decided he'd done all he could do, and instead he'd ask his sergeant if he could get involved with something else. It was pointless spending any more time in here.

As he went to leave, the floorboard creaked below his feet. Nothing unusual in itself — they'd been creaking every time he walked over them — but this time it had the effect of sparking a thought in his mind.

Apart from one room, which had a concrete floor, the others in this building all had wooden boards. The boarded rooms were a good foot or two higher than the concrete one. Indeed, you had to step up into the boarded rooms and down into the concrete-floored one. But why had these rooms been raised? He could see no logical reason for it. It made getting through doorways a nightmare. And aside from that, there were the other odd noises he'd been hearing. He'd put it down to the generator in the field nearby, or perhaps just the sorts of noises that old damp buildings made. But there was something telling him the faint murmur wasn't quite right.

He took a screwdriver from his box of tricks, knelt down and tried to prise back one of the loosest floorboards. It was taking quite some effort, but it was shifting. He'd just about managed to lift it up enough to slide his fingers underneath the gap and give it a proper lift, which meant he'd be able to lift the two neighbouring floorboards.

But he didn't need to.

As the floorboard lifted, he saw the milky, yellowy whites of the pair of eyes looking back up at him, blinking as the light cut across them.

53

Wendy heard the sound of Culverhouse's office phone clattering back into its cradle. A moment later, the door flew open and he came marching over to her.

'Knight. Where's Kümmel? Has he been released yet?'

'Yeah, a few moments ago,' Wendy said, noting the look of panic and excitement on his face. 'There's a patrol car dropping him back. Why?'

'Shit. Grab your coat.'

Before Wendy could say anything, Culverhouse was jogging towards the stairs.

'What is it?' Wendy said, when she finally caught up with him in the car park.

'There's been a discovery at the farm. A fucking big one. That medical centre? A PC thought there was something weird about it, so he pulled up the floorboards. He found Amy Kemp and Ben Gallagher, bound and gagged.'

'Alive?' Wendy asked, getting into the passenger seat of Culverhouse's car and closing the door.

'Barely. Amy's in a worse state than Ben, but neither of them are looking too rosy. They reckon there could be more, too. They reckon that's where the bodies are.'

Wendy couldn't quite believe what she was hearing. 'Shit. Are you serious?'

'Afraid so,' Culverhouse said, turning left out of the car park and putting his right foot to the floor.

'But won't the officers at the farm intercept him when he gets there?' Wendy asked.

'Yes, but I want to be the one to nab him. They were going to suggest calling off the search. Fucking good job they didn't.'

Wendy had to admit that had Culverhouse not joined CID, he could have made a decent traffic cop. His high-speed driving under pressure had often impressed her, and she never felt unsafe with him at the wheel. And with the speed he was travelling at, it was a good job too.

As Jack ate up the road in front of them, Wendy's thoughts turned to what they would find when they got there. She could only imagine the scene, discovering what Ben and Amy had been through. And all the time they'd been sitting in an interview room with Father Joseph and his arrogant solicitor, he'd known exactly what had gone on. He'd almost convinced her of his innocence. Not quite, but she'd had her moments. He was a calm and confident man. Clinically a psychopath, Wendy thought. Not the comic-book interpretation of the word — a babbling screaming maniac, but a person who has no empathy or remorse, and instead feeds off their own ego and sense of self-importance. She always found people like that both scary and remarkably interesting.

It scared her to know that even she, an experienced Detective Sergeant, could have come close to being sucked in by someone like Father Joseph. He had completely and utterly believed that he was in complete control of the situation and that he'd come out smelling of roses. He'd seemed almost affronted that the police had had the nerve to even investigate him.

But that would all change now. He'd have one hell of a shock when he got back to Hilltop Farm.

She thought of all the people who'd been affected by Father Joseph Kümmel's ego-driven life. The Bens, the Amys, the Sandras. There'd be more, she knew. And the saddest stories wouldn't be from those who'd escaped and were able to tell the tale. They'd be from those who'd died at Hilltop Farm or were still living there, oblivious to the crimes that had gone on around them and still unfailingly faithful to Father Joseph and his church.

She pulled her mobile phone out of her pocket, unlocked it and fired off a text to Steve Wing.

Any news from Dorset on finding Sandra K?

54

Lulworth Cove was a beautiful place all year round, but it seemed particularly engaging and serene today. The late morning sun had burnt through the mist and the smooth azure sky looked polished and ready for the rest of the day. Whatever that day might bring.

Sandra had parked her car in a car park a short walk away. She'd been down here yesterday, too, but it hadn't felt right. Maybe she'd been tired after the drive, but it didn't seem to be the place she recognised and loved. Today, though, was different.

Today, it felt like a new world. It seemed so far disconnected from yesterday to be almost a completely different world. Anyone else might've seen that as a sign of new beginnings, of a fresh start. But Sandra knew there could be no new beginnings, no fresh start. Something like she'd been through was always just the beginning of the end.

The torment would always be there. Things like that

never went away. They had a lasting, damaging impression on your psyche. When your trust, your belief and your faith are abused in such a way, how can you ever expect to trust again, believe again, have faith again? No blue sky could ever make Sandra want to live in a world like that.

But something had changed. She knew that much. Maybe it was just a sense, a spiritual connection. But the colour of the sky that morning and the sound of the waves crashing against the rock told her that a page had been turned. A new chapter had begun. The story was over. She looked down at the rocks below, watching the water crash over them, the spume calling to her, talking to her. It seemed to be telling her everything was alright. Whispered messages revealed the truth.

She'd never heard the sounds so vibrant, never seen the sky so bright. It marked the turning point. But for her, there could be no turning. She couldn't go back and there was no way of moving on, either. She'd forever be rooted in what happened, in what was still happening. Ghosts did not simply disappear.

She looked down at the rocks again, and listened as the white spume and crashing waves called to her.

Slowly, she looked up and stepped forward towards the edge, her toes hanging out over the precipice.

She took a deep breath, looked back down at the waves, and answered their call.

55

They arrived at Hilltop Farm barely a few minutes later. Culverhouse wrenched the handbrake on and jumped out of the car before Wendy had even registered that they'd stopped.

She could see Father Joseph had arrived back at the farm maybe less than a minute before they had. He still had a look of shock on his face as the uniformed officers detained him at the gate and informed him that he was being re-arrested on suspicion of murder, conspiracy to murder and of perverting the course of justice.

'We meet again, Father J,' Culverhouse bellowed as he walked up behind him. 'Who'd've known it'd be so soon?'

'Would you care to tell me what this is all about, Detective Chief Inspector?' Father Joseph replied, his face belying the calm, composed air his voice held.

'Certainly,' Culverhouse replied. 'All in good time.

Now if you wouldn't mind waiting here with these officers, I'll be back in a few moments.'

He beckoned for Wendy to follow him and the uniformed PC, who led them towards the medical centre.

Inside, the air seemed to be different to outside. It was heavier somehow. The PC led them to the threshold of the main room, where the floorboards had all been taken up. The surface underneath showed a number of holes, recesses in the concrete that were probably five feet deep and four feet wide. Jack reckoned there must be a good dozen of them in here alone. But his eyes were drawn to the areas of concrete that didn't have holes — the areas where fresher concrete, of a different colour, had been smoothed over the top.

'Ben Gallagher was found in this one,' the PC said, pointing to one of the holes, 'and Amy Kemp in this one. Amy's in no fit state to talk at the moment, but Ben seems mostly just dehydrated and worn. He said he was told to drink a poison, to end his own life. He refused, so he was bound and gagged and put in one of the holes.'

'Christ,' Wendy said. 'And what were they going to do then?'

The PC shrugged. 'If you ask me, I reckon we're going to find bodies under the rest of this. My theory is if people wouldn't take the cyanide and kill themselves, they were put into one of these pits to die naturally. Then they'd come in and fill in the hole with concrete.'

Wendy stood, stunned. 'Shit. But there must be...'

'I know,' the PC said. 'There's loads of them. Doesn't even bear thinking about.'

Outside, Father Joseph stood patiently with two officers. By now, he'd managed to regain his look of composure and complete confidence. Wendy couldn't see how he was going to wriggle his way out of this one, though.

'Thank you, officers,' Culverhouse called over. 'We'll deal with this one from here.'

He waited until the two uniformed PCs had disappeared from sight, then he looked Father Joseph Kümmel in the eye.

'I've seen some stuff in my time,' he said. 'But that just about tops the lot. Go on, then. Give us your pathetic explanation.'

'I'm not quite sure what I'm meant to be explaining,' Father Joseph replied.

'The pits. Ben Gallagher and Amy Kemp were found inside concrete pits under the floorboards in your medical centre. *Your* medical centre.'

'The church's medical centre,' Father Joseph replied.

'Interesting. If someone had said to me that people had been found bound and gagged on my property, my first response would've been some sort of shock. I might even ask if they were alive or dead. I wouldn't immediately jump on the defensive and try to deflect blame. Why did you do that?'

Father Joseph smiled. 'Detective Chief Inspector, are

you accusing me of a crime here? A number of people live in this community. I cannot be held responsible for their actions.'

Culverhouse took a step closer towards him. 'So what if I were to tell you that we've got a witness, perhaps two, who are willing to testify that you tried to get them to drink cyanide. And that when they refused, you had them thrown into those pits.' He could see the flicker in Father Joseph's eyes. 'Ah. You didn't know that bit, did you? You didn't know they were still alive. Tough cookies, Ben and Amy. Ben's even talking. Can't shut him up. Attempting assisted suicide? That's quite something.'

Father Joseph flared his nostrils. 'Never in my life have my hands ended the life of another person. If the Lord chooses to take these lives, that is His choice to make. I am simply his servant.'

Culverhouse stepped forward again, his nose almost touching Father Joseph's. 'Interesting deflection. I suppose God has provided a great alibi for you, hasn't he? Saves having to take responsibility yourself. But then again, it was all one big scam wasn't it? Admit it, Kümmel. Your power's just crumbled away. Now you're nothing but a sad, pathetic old man.'

Wendy watched as Father Joseph's face contorted, a split second before he launched himself at Culverhouse. Culverhouse stepped to the side, wrenched Father Joseph's arm behind his back and read him his rights.

56

The atmosphere amongst the group assembled in the Prince Albert was slightly different to what it'd traditionally been following the handover of a case to the CPS. Often, there'd be a celebratory atmosphere; a feeling of a job well done. This time, though, there was a huge undercurrent of regret. Regret that they'd not been able to apprehend Father Joseph sooner, that they'd not had information earlier which could have saved more lives.

It wasn't often that the scale and nature of a killer's crimes was discovered only at the end of a case. It was the upside-down nature of the Hilltop Farm investigation that had thrown a few people off kilter. Regardless, though, a decision to charge was a decision to charge. It would now be largely down to the courts to ensure that Father Joseph Kümmel saw justice.

Culverhouse had, as tradition dictated, bought the first round and was readily letting the others know that he had, of course, had suspicions about Father Joseph all along. DC Ryan Mackenzie entered the pub, her rucksack slung over one shoulder, a hand-knitted beanie hat pulled over her head.

'Drink?' Culverhouse said, by way of greeting.

'Great, thanks,' Ryan replied. 'I'll have a pint of Foster's.'

Culverhouse looked at her for a moment, but chose to say nothing and instead went back to the bar to buy her drink.

'Alright?' Wendy asked Ryan as she sat down.

'Yeah I'm good. Had a couple of things I wanted to finish off. Give me less to do in the morning. Mandy should be joining us in a bit. She'll be leaving work in a few minutes.'

Wendy smiled. She was looking forward to meeting Ryan's partner, but she was more looking forward to seeing the awkwardness of Jack Culverhouse as he tried to politely make conversation with a lesbian couple.

'Shame about ol' Sandra Kaporsky,' Steve said, somehow internally sensing that a positive atmosphere needed extinguishing.

'Mmmm,' Wendy replied, not wanting to delve too far into the negative. 'Just goes to show how deeply things like that can affect people. It's tragic.'

'What's happened?' Ryan asked, taking off her coat.

'Chucked herself off a cliff,' Steve replied through a mouthful of peanuts before Wendy could answer.

'Dorset Police found the body of a woman on the rocks

at Lulworth Cove,' Wendy explained a little more delicately. 'It was identified as being Sandra.'

Frank Vine quietly stood up and made his way over to the bar, where Culverhouse was paying for Ryan's drink.

'Guv, can I have a word?' he said.

'Have as many as you like, Frank. I've got nothing to use them for.'

'Right. Look, I've been thinking. Well, we both have. Me and Lorraine. We're neither of us getting any younger. Since her mother left us a bit of money, we've been spending more time up in the Lake District. We've both realised how much we like it up there. Her pension's already kicked in and is doing alright. I reckon mine'd give us a decent whack, especially if we sold our place down here and had a lower cost of living. Up there, see, you can get a place for half what you can down here. I reckon if we—'

'Frank, will you get to the fucking point? I've got a dentist's appointment next Thursday.'

'Right. Well the thing is, I'm thinking of taking early retirement.'

Culverhouse looked at him for a moment. 'Early? You must be about eighty-five.'

'Cheeky f... I'm fifty-nine, guv.'

'Are you fuck.'

'I am. Honest,' Frank said, looking offended.

'Christ. Fountain of Youth wasn't kind to you, was it?' Culverhouse replied.

Frank looked down at his feet for a moment. 'Hardly surprising. I've worked hard all these years.'

Culverhouse almost choked on his beer. 'Worked hard? Yeah, I think I even saw you make your own coffee once. 1994, it must've been.' He put a hand on Frank's shoulder. 'Seriously, though, mate. You'll be a big loss to the team if you do decide to go. I hope you don't, but if you do I totally understand. I'd do the same if I could.'

'You could,' Frank said. 'You must have enough put away by now.'

Culverhouse chuckled. 'Not about the money, though, is it? Not for me. Truth be told, they could've forgotten to pay me for the last six months and I wouldn't have noticed.' The mention of time passing had him thinking of Helen. He wondered where she was now, if she was out of hospital and where she would've gone. He'd long decided it was best that he didn't know. The twenty thousand Danish krone in her back pocket would keep his conscience at bay for now.

The pair made their way back over to the group. A few minutes later, the door opened and an attractive young woman walked in. She didn't seem to be familiar with the place, but had turned plenty of heads on entering.

'Fuck a duck,' Culverhouse said to Steve Wing, elbowing him in the arm. 'Get a load of that.'

'Blimey,' came Steve's response. 'She must be lost. You don't get lookers like that round here.' As Steve was speaking, the woman looked at the group, smiled and walked towards them. 'Bloody hell. I wish I'd worn clean pants.'

Ryan stood up as the woman approached, and kissed her on the cheek. 'Guys, this is Mandy. Mandy, this is Wendy, Steve, Frank, Debbie and Jack.'

'Hi,' Mandy said, lifting her hand in a small wave.

'Hi,' Culverhouse said, extending his hand towards her. 'I'm Jack.' He looked at Ryan as he said the last word, the inference being that he wasn't used to DCs being quite so informal.

Mandy shook his hand, then sat down.

Wendy looked around at the group and exchanged a look with Debbie Weston. They were both thinking exactly the same thing: it'd be a thing of beauty to sit and watch Jack, Steve and Frank try to make politically-correct conversation.

Jack, though, had his mind in other places. He looked down at his mobile phone and read the text message again. It was from Emily.

Don't worry about the whole dinner with Ethan thing. Said he doesn't want to see me anymore. Feeling down but don't worry about rushing back. I'll be ok. See you later x

He stood up and took his coat from the back of his chair. 'I've got to go,' he said. 'Sorry.' He looked at his colleagues and sensed some tension coming from the direction of Ryan. 'It's stuff at home. Sorry. Honestly, it's been lovely to meet you, Mandy. Can we all do this again another night?'

'Course,' Mandy replied, smiling. 'I'm never going to say no to more drinks.'

57

Wendy was nursing a slight hangover the next morning, but she didn't mind too much. They'd been successful in arresting and charging Father Joseph Kümmel, and last night's celebratory session in the Prince Albert had gone down well. Mandy had got on well with everyone, she thought. That was particularly impressive considering the fact that everyone else there was a police officer, and at least two of them were politically incorrect dinosaurs.

Culverhouse had seemed genuinely apologetic that he'd had to leave early, too. Wendy got the sense that it was nothing to do with Ryan and Mandy, and that he'd had other things on his mind. She hoped they knew that, too.

She jumped a little as Culverhouse appeared behind her at her desk, announcing his arrival with a 'Morning'.

'Sorry, made me jump,' she replied, hoping he hadn't heard her slight yelp.

'Come and see me in my office when you've got a sec,' he said. 'Got something I want to talk to you about.'

Wendy thought to herself for a moment and wondered what it might be. They'd made enough mistakes during the investigation into Hilltop Farm, but she couldn't think of anything that hadn't already been addressed. Ben Gallagher was recovering well at his brother's house, Amy Kemp was due to leave hospital in the next couple of days and work was beginning on recovering and identifying the bodies buried beneath the medical centre. There would be one hell of a lot of work for social services to get involved with, too. A lot of people living at Hilltop Farm wouldn't want to leave, regardless of what had gone on, such was the level of brainwashing they'd undergone over the years. And those who did want to leave and return to conventional society would have to integrate somehow, having spent years isolated from their families and friends. She couldn't even begin to imagine how they'd go about that, or what measures and facilities would be in place to help them.

She made her way into Culverhouse's office and closed the door behind her. She stood at his desk while she waited for him to finish replying to an email — which took a little while with Culverhouse's two-fingered typing — and wondered what this was all about.

'How do you think things are going?' the DCI asked, eventually.

'Uh, fine,' Wendy replied, not quite sure what he meant.

He nodded and pursed his lips. 'Good. Good. I think so too.'

She sensed that the tone of the meeting was meant to be positive. Most people, when having to deliver bad news, would look as awkward as Culverhouse did now. He was absolutely fine with delivering bad news, though. It was praise he struggled with. She decided to take the bull by the horns and put him out of his misery.

'What's this all about?' she asked.

'Well, the structure of the team is changing a bit, as you know. With Luke gone, and Ryan coming in, and with everyone going on above and at Milton House...'

'And with Frank retiring,' Wendy offered.

'Yeah. Well, I wouldn't look too far into that. He's been going on about retiring since his first day. The day Frank Vine retires is the day I run skipping out of Milton House holding Malcolm Pope's hand.'

'I dunno. He seemed pretty set on the idea.'

'Either way,' Culverhouse said, shuffling in his seat, 'we're a bit DS-heavy, if you see what I mean.'

Wendy's heart caught in her throat. He had a point — there were three detective sergeants on the team, including her. So what, was he having her transferred elsewhere? And why her? Steve Wing and Frank Vine were next to useless compared to her. Wouldn't it be better off having them transferred? Or letting Frank take his early retirement? Of course, Frank and Steve were Culverhouse's lapdogs. That probably had something to do with it. All these thoughts — and more — rushed through Wendy's head as she tried to make sense of what she was being told.

Culverhouse's next words jolted her out of her panic.

'I want you to take your Inspector's exams.'

Wendy found herself unable to speak for a moment. 'Sorry, what?'

'I said I want you to take your Inspector's exams. You've been on the team a while now and you've shown yourself to be... alright... at managing people. And when I've not been around and you've taken charge of things you've managed not to fuck too much up.'

She smiled. Coming from Culverhouse, that was a major compliment.

If she was honest with herself, she'd never really thought about moving upwards in her career. Deep down, she knew why that was. Her own father had made Detective Inspector. That was the rank he'd been when he'd died. To her, she felt she always had the responsibility to remain one step behind him. He'd had his life taken from him far too young, and should have been able to progress much further. But he hadn't been able to. To reach the same rank as her father — and potentially outrank him — would somehow feel as though she was betraying him.

'I know what you're thinking,' Culverhouse said. 'But try not to let it affect you. You should be proud of yourself, like he'd be proud of you.'

Wendy looked at him and smiled. And in that moment she knew he was right.

GET MORE OF MY BOOKS FREE!

Thank you for reading *In the Name of the Father*. I hope it was as much fun for you as it was for me writing it.

To say thank you, I'd like to invite you to my exclusive *VIP Club*, and give you some of my books and short stories for FREE. All members of my VIP Club have access to FREE, exclusive books and short stories which aren't available anywhere else.

You'll also get access to all of my new releases at a bargain-basement price before they're available anywhere else. Joining is absolutely FREE and you can leave at any time, no questions asked. To join the club, head to adamcroft.net/vip-club **and two free books will be sent to you straight away!**

If you enjoyed the book, please do leave a review on

the site you bought it from. Reviews mean an awful lot to writers and they help us to find new readers more than almost anything else. It would be very much appreciated.

I love hearing from my readers, too, so please do feel free to get in touch with me. You can contact me via my website, on Twitter @adamcroft and you can 'like' my Facebook page at facebook.com/adamcroftbooks.

For more information, visit my website: adamcroft.net

KNIGHT & CULVERHOUSE RETURN IN 'WITH A VENGEANCE'

OUT NOW

Eleven years ago. A bungled armed robbery led by career criminal Freddie Galloway leaves a police officer shot in the face, fighting for his life.

Present day. The shooter is released from prison, hell bent on revenge. That night, Freddie Galloway leaps to his death to escape a blazing inferno in his country mansion.

With arson confirmed as the cause of the fire, Mildenheath CID are left battling a web of lies as they delve deep into the dark underbelly of Mildenheath's criminal underworld.

But what they discover will be enough to shock them to the core.

Turn the page to read the first chapter...

WITH A VENGEANCE

CHAPTER 1

Eleven years ago

The night was still. The four men held their breath. The loudest sound was the the pulse of blood in their own ears.

The back of the Transit van was dark but for the beam emanating from Footloose's torch. The other three watched as Footloose's hand signalled the countdown: five fingers, then four, three, two, one. With a nod, he turned and pushed open the rear doors of the van, the other three men following close behind.

Within seconds, they were inside the industrial unit. Their inside man had done his job and would be paid handsomely.

That was always the trickiest part of jobs like this — until it got to this moment, you never quite knew whether your man on the inside was stringing you along or not. They'd all heard of huge plans that had gone wrong because their contact had gone to the law or, worse, arranged to double-cross them. But this was all going perfectly to plan.

Once they were inside, Headache got to work on the on-duty security guard, pinning him to the ground before he'd managed to grab hold of his radio and sound the alarm.

The guard was a tough cookie. Much bigger than they'd been led to believe, but it only took Headache a few seconds to live up to his name, delivering a skull-splitting headbutt to the man's face, knocking him unconscious. With the guard now a little easier to manipulate, Headache and Bruno frisked him down, removing his tools and equipment, before gagging him and handcuffing him to the copper pipework.

'Oi, Footloose. We've got a problem here!' Peter yelled from inside the office. They only ever used their nicknames when on a job. They couldn't risk blowing their real identities, and they never knew who was listening.

'What do you mean "problem"?' Footloose replied, seemingly unruffled. Despite the calm tone of his voice, Headache and Bruno knew when Footloose was upset. Their years of knowing him and working with him meant they would realise a couple of seconds before most people. That still wouldn't give them enough time to get out of his way, though.

Footloose walked through to the office and looked down at Peter, who was crouched down by the safe.

'It's not the model he told us it was,' Peter said. 'I'm not tooled up for this one.'

Footloose looked him in the eye and spoke calmly. 'What do you mean you're not tooled up?'

'I mean, this needs extra gear. I can't get into this with the tools I've brought. I'm going to need—'

Peter's sentence was cut short by Footloose lifting him up by the front of his overalls and pinning him to the wall. He could hear the fabric ripping and tearing as it struggled to hold his weight, his feet dangling a good few inches off the ground.

'You're a bloody safe breaker,' Footloose yelled, spittle flying through the mere millimetres that separated their faces. He pulled Peter away from the wall and slammed him back against it with each word. 'You. Break. Safes. Get it?'

Before Peter could reply, Footloose's attention was taken by the distant sound of sirens.

'Footloose! There's sirens!' Bruno called from outside the office.

'I can hear that,' came the reply, as he threw Peter to the ground. 'Now what the fuck's going on?'

He could see immediately that none of the others had any clue.

'They're getting closer. They're coming here!' Bruno said.

Footloose knew he had to make his decision quickly.

'We need to split. Headache, back out the way we came. You too, you useless prick,' he said through gritted teeth, picking Peter up and shoving him over towards Headache. 'Bruno, with me.' We'll take the fire escape.'

The men nodded and made to do as they were told, before Footloose gave them one last instruction.

'And remember. If there's even the slightest possibility that anyone's following you to the safe house — even the tiniest fraction of a chance — you abandon. Alright?'

The men nodded again, and Footloose gestured for them to get moving.

It took three shoulder-barges for Bruno to shake the back door free of its hinges, before he and Footloose clambered up the metal stairs, jumped the low wall and ran off into the woods behind the industrial estate.

Towards the front of the unit, Peter and Headache were ready to break for the exit. As they rounded the corner and started to run towards the van, their attention was taken by a voice shouting from the darkness. Peter carried straight on to the van, but Headache stopped and turned towards the voice.

A man jogged out of the shadows, clearly almost out of breath, his policeman's uniform reflecting under the streetlights.

'Get on the floor,' the policeman said, struggling to talk between breaths. 'Get down. Hands behind your head.'

'Yeah, as if,' Headache replied, turning to join Peter back at the van before the rest of the cops arrived. He could see this guy had no weapons, no truncheon, nothing. Just a beat cop who'd heard the call go out over the radio and been unlucky enough to get here first.

'Wait,' the policeman called out. 'I know you. Don't I?'

'Headache! Get in the van!'

Headache looked at the policeman for a moment. 'No. Sorry. You're mistaken.'

'Yeah I do. You're—'

'Headache! Now!'

'Yeah. Last September. The Moulson Arms. I know who you are.'

'Headache! I'm going if you don't get in the van right now!'

Headache's jaw started to tense as he stretched out his hand, then quickly dipped it into his inside jacket pocket, pulled out the Makarov pistol and raised it in front of him, the barrel pointed directly at the policeman's head.

'Jesus Christ, Headache! No!' Peter yelled, by now revving the van's engine and beeping the horn to get his attention.

Headache swallowed, narrowed his eyes, and pulled the trigger.

Want to read on?

Visit adamcroft.net/book/with-a-vengeance to grab your copy.

Printed in June 2022
by Rotomail Italia S.p.A., Vignate (MI) - Italy